THE
UNDERTAKER'S ASSISTANT

James D. Farrell

ORIGINAL WRITING

All rights reserved. No part of this publication may be reproduced
in any form or by any means—graphic, electronic or mechanical,
including photocopying, recording, taping or information storage and
retrieval systems—without the prior written permission of the author.

978-1-908282-84-2

A CIP catalogue for this book is available from the National Library.

Published by Original Writing Ltd., Dublin, 2011.

Printed by Cahill Printers Limited, Dublin.

This book is dedicated to the memory of

Colm Francis Farrell

Contents

PIG'S FEET

Eddie Kelly was in a deep sleep snoring gently as the early morning sunlight shone brightly through the tattered curtains of his bedroom window. He was dreaming again. It was the same dream. He was in a jungle somewhere strange and far away and she was there: the same beautiful young girl, dark skinned with long silky black hair. She was smiling at him. As he slowly reached out his hand to touch her naked body he was rudely awoken from his wonderful reverie by his father Seamy shouting from the bottom of the stairs, "Get up out of dat feckin bed yeh lazy bastard or you'll be late for work again."

After a few minutes, staring blankly at the smoke-stained ceiling, Eddie reached down and picked up his trousers which were lying crumpled in a heap on the bare floor boards and fumbled in his pocket for a Woodbine cigarette. Two left. He placed the overflowing ashtray on his chest, lit his cigarette and lay quietly on the bed inhaling deeply. He liked to have a smoke before he got out of bed in the morning. As he enjoyed the cigarette he began to feel slightly better. Then it dawned on him – happy days; it was Friday, Eddie's favourite day of the week.

Roll on tonight, he thought as he finished his cigarette – his big night out. He jumped out of bed at the thought of it and dressed in his shabby black suit. He headed quickly to the toilet, urinated and threw cold water on his face and went quickly down the stairs.

The living room smelt of sweet cider and stale tobacco smoke. His father, having received his unemployment benefit the day before, had been up all night chain-smoking Sweet Afton cigarettes, scrutinising the racing paper and drinking cider. "Eddie isn't it grand me getting yeh dat job with Shaky Shanahan, yeh know me unemployment benefit doesn't go very far on the drink or the odd bet on the horses. Are yeh not proud now dat you're the breadwinner in the family what with Paddy gone." Seamy sat at the table chewing slowly on a plate of cold pig's feet. Eddie felt sick at the sight of the trotters. Seamy caught the look of disgust on his son's face.

"Eddie, Eddie, do yeh see that little piggy bastard," he said, solemnly pointing at the table. "Do yeh know what Eddie; he was a dirty little fucker so he was. He wiped his greasy hands in the newspaper and continued. "Do yeh know why? Well, I'll tell yeh why so I will; the dirty little bastard never cut his bleedin toenails. Eddie, for the love of Sweet Jaysus will yeh ever look at the state of his bleedin toenails; they're disgusting so they are, and he was a hairy bastard too. Eddie will yeh ever look at the feckin hair on his toes?"

Eddie glanced at the pig's feet. Christ, his da was right: long curling toenails and hairy toes – disgusting. He looked away quickly when he felt his stomach turn.

"Will yeh have a cut of scald, Eddie?"

"Da yeh know I don't like drinking me tea without milk. Where's Ma?"

"Where do yeh think she is? Up at the church again," his father replied."Eatin the feckin altar rails. She went up to half seven mass as usual."

Eddie picked up his battered top hat and without speaking to his father walked out the door and ran down the narrow path across the fields towards Finglas village to catch the eight o'clock bus into the city centre and Shaky Shanahan's funeral home where he worked as an undertaker's assistant.

"Good morning to yeh Eddie," said the bus conductor as he climbed aboard. "Heading for the dead centre of town?" Wherever Eddie went he got the same old boring funeral jokes. "Hey Eddie, yeh know what son" the bus conductor continued "a fella would die to get a job like yours so he would." Every old wag would go on and on with the undertaker jibes. But Eddie knew there was nothing funny about working with the corpses of the Dublin slums. As usual the bus was full with standing room only, the passenger's packed in like sardines and all heading for work in the city centre, the smell of body sweat and stale tobacco pervading the air of the crowded bus.

As the packed bus passed Finglas Primary School Eddie looked at the grey squat building and remembered how his older brother Paddy use to pick him up after school when he was on leave from the Irish army on his motorbike – a shining new blue coloured Yamaha 90.He remembered well that day a few years ago when he was been bullied by Spud Murphy and his gang. As he lay on the hard concrete of the school yard crying, with a bloody nose and grazed knee, he looked up and saw Paddy standing there like a God: six feet tall and dressed in his green army uniform with the shiny brass buttons. Spud Murphy and his gang ran off as soon as they saw Paddy. Eddie was so proud of his big brother in his uniform. Paddy picked him up off the ground and said, "Listen little brother for Christ sake will yeh ever stop you're crying." He wiped his baby brother's eyes with his handkerchief and lifted him up in his strong arms. Then he said softly, "Listen little brother, I'll always be there to look after you so I will, I'll always mind yeh so I will. So if you're ever scared or in trouble just call out the magic words – Paddy! Paddy! – And no matter where I am I'll come for yeh little fella okay? Always remember the magic words."Eddie never forgot the magic words. His brother lifted him gently onto the saddle of his shiny new Yamaha and they drove home with Paddy's big strong arms holding him tightly in front of him. He loved riding on Paddy's motorbike; the noise of the engine; the feel of the wind blowing in his face and, most of all, Paddy holding him tight. He felt so warm and so secure. Strong arms and gentle heart – that was his big brother. He was the only good thing in his life. God, he missed Paddy so much, he made him feel secure and gave him all the things his father never did.

Eddie glanced quickly back at the school and for a second imagined Paddy sitting outside on his motorbike waiting for him to come running out the gates when the bell rang. But Paddy was gone now and nothing was right anymore. They had barely enough money to feed themselves; his father's drinking himself to death and his mother's going bloody bonkers and heading rapidly for Grange Gorman mental asylum with her obsession about getting a fancy grave and a big marble statue for Paddy. *God, I wish I had the guts to rob a bank*, he thought, as the packed number forty bus trundled slowly towards Dublin city centre.

The funeral parlour was a rundown business located in a mew's lane at the rear of Finlater's Place in the centre of the city. Shaky had inherited the business some years before when his elderly father died suddenly from a heart attack. It was an old-fashioned business and just about able to compete with the modern undertakers and was the last firm in the city to have a horse-drawn hearse. But it was cheap and very popular with the poor of the city who went to Shaky to bury their dead. He was even known to provide the funeral service for the price of a few drinks.

Shaky was a dwarf of a man in his mid sixties with long greasy grey hair, a flushed face and big red nose from the copious amount of whiskey he drank – he was always half-drunk. He smelt bad and when people complained he would reply, "Work with the dead, smell like the dead." He never married and lived in a small room at the back of the funeral parlour and it was rumoured that he slept in a coffin at night. But he was a kind man who respected Eddie and treated him like a son.

Shaky Shanahan and Eddie were well known around the city – skinny, glum-faced Eddie, round glasses and long brown hair, a Woodbine cigarette hanging from his mouth, walking beside the diminutive round figure of Shaky Shanahan, a perpetual smile on his red face; the pair of them wearing shabby, black, oversized old-fashioned dress suits and battered top hats which Shaky had bought second-hand at the flea market up beside Christchurch Cathedral. Passers-by would laugh at the sight of the pair. 'Lanky and Large was the name given to the undertaker and his assistant by the people of Dublin. The odd wag would say, "Jaysus isn't the big lanky fucker a dead ringer for Dracula," ridiculing Eddie's sombre expression. In fact Shaky Shanahans was the only undertakers in Dublin where you were guaranteed a good laugh at the funeral. But Shaky Shanahan was a generous man who never refused to do a good turn for anyone no matter who they were. Many a pauper he buried without payment. He refused no one.

THE STARRY PLOUGH

Bridie Kelly lit a candle to The Sacred Heart of Mercy and sat at the back of the cold, near empty church. She went to early mass every morning without fail; she liked the stillness and solitude of the church in the cold light of the mornings. She would offer up her prayers for the souls of her departed family: her poor mother and father, Christy and Nora Doyle, and for her first-born son Paddy. Although Bridie had never met her dad (she was born after he was killed), not a day passed without her praying for him. Christy Doyle had been a tram driver with the Dublin Metropolitan Tram Company but his wages were barely enough to feed his family and pay the rent on their small house in Ringsend. The wages were poor for all Dublin workers and poverty and hardship were widespread throughout the city. Christy joined Jim Larkin's trade union movement which organised the workers to strike for better wages and conditions. The whole of Dublin came to a standstill and violent clashes occurred across the city as the police tried to break up protesting strikers and many people were injured and killed. After weeks of starvation and misery the strike ended in failure and the worker's returned to work. The bosses issued a decree stating that no worker was to remain a member of the trade union and if they did so they would be locked out from their place of work. The worker's refused and the Great Lock Out began. Scab labour was brought in and violence and mayhem was widespread across the city of Dublin. Alarmed at the violence against their members the trade unions organised the workers into an armed group to defend themselves and the Citizen's Army was born. Christy Doyle was one of the first volunteers to join the Dublin Brigade of the new militant labour movement. He came out with James Connolly in the Easter Rising of 1916 under the Starry Plough flag to fight against the English and was shot dead defending a barricade in the General Post Office in O'Connell's Street. Bridie was born six month's later.

She was obsessed with the memory of her father. Her mother had told her how her father had walked out of their house in Ringsend on Easter Monday 1916 dressed in the uniform of the Citizen's Army and carrying an old German rifle with a bandolier over his shoulder with twenty rounds of ammunition. He kissed his pregnant wife and then his young son Sean and left never to return. His last words to his wife were, "Nora don't make it hard for me now yeh know I have to go. It's me duty to follow big Jem Connolly and strike a blow for the Dublin workers against the English for our freedom, for the future of our children."

As Christy walked down the street he turned once and waved a final goodbye to his family. Nora knew he wasn't coming back; women knew these things instinctively. She was however shocked when a young boy dressed in an oversized uniform and struggling to carry a rifle that was bigger than him joined Christy at the corner of the street. It was Brendan Mackey, a young apprentice fitter from the tram company. He was fourteen years old. *Jaysus, Mary and Joseph*, she thought. *That Jim Connolly has a lot to answer for bringing youngsters out to their deaths.*

The weeks passed and Christy never came home and one day the local Dublin Metropolitan policeman, a kind elderly man, told Nora that he had heard a rumour that her husband had been shot and killed in the General Post Office by an English soldier and was buried up in Arbour Hill Military Cemetery. But she heard nothing officially. No one came to tell her anything, not even an English Officer in a fancy uniform – nobody. Day after day she would sit at the bottom of the stairs holding her young son Sean and staring at the front door waiting patiently for a knock that would never come. She was hungry, her child was hungry. She was pregnant, what would she do? Each long lonely night she would lie in bed with her young son and cry herself to sleep.

She went to the local priest who wrote to General Maxwell, commander of the English forces in Dublin, to try and get Christy's body released from military custody. The General refused; he didn't want any more Fenian martyrs. The bodies of the volunteers were buried in Arbour Hill Military Cemetery and that's where the remains of her father had lain for the past fifty years or more.

Nora never found out what happened to the young Brendan Mackey. She often thought about going out to his house in Booterstown to find out if he'd been hurt or even worse but she was afraid that his parent's would blame Christy for their son becoming involved in the Citizen's Army. She couldn't bear to have anyone say a bad word about her husband or tarnish his sacred memory.

But she had nothing to worry about. When the bedraggled Citizen Army Volunteers surrendered after a couple of days of hard fighting in the G.P.O. an English Officer looked at the pathetic figure of Brendan Mackey stumbling from the burning ruins with his blackened face and blazing eyes. He was shocked then slightly embarrassed. *Is this what we've been fighting?* He thought. He slapped the boy soldier on the head, made him take off the oversized uniform and sent him home to his family.

Nora was destitute and had no choice but to move in with Christy's two unmarried sisters, Florrrie and Greta, two retired national school teachers, who lived in a terraced house in Bath Avenue in Sandymount and it was here that Bridie was born and reared. Bridie lived in the house with Florrie and Greta until she married Seamy Kelly. He was so dashing and handsome; he swept her off her feet. He was a bus conductor with C.I.E. on the number ten to Sandymount; ten was always her lucky number. He was so full of life then – her knight in shining armour even though it was only a shabby navy blue busman's uniform with the shiny peaked hat. God she loved a man in a uniform; it made them look so gallant, like her father must have looked all those years before in his Citizen's Army uniform. Seamy rescued her from the dark prison that was her home in Sandymount and they were married in the Star of the Sea Church in Sandymount on a beautiful summer's day. Father Burke had said, "For better or for worse." As it turned out there was very little of the better but plenty of the worse.

They rented a small flat in D'Olier Street in the city centre with no electricity or bathroom but at least the rent was low. It was all they could afford. Things started to go wrong after they were married and Paddy was born. Seamy just couldn't cope with the responsibility of family life. He started to drink heavily and was sacked for stealing bus fares. She soon realised that he was a child not a man. She remembered her mother Nora's words: "Love thrives or love dies." No truer words. Women were the strong ones, men the weak ones.

Maybe it's the mothers that make Irish men weak – you can't blame the English for everything! When she got pregnant with Paddy she thought things could change and Seamy might start acting like a man and face up to his responsibilities but he only got worse. She began to despise him – a good for nothing waster. All she wanted was a man to give her what her father never did: to come home from work and hold her, to love her and make her feel secure and special – Daddy's little girl. Every Easter she would make a point of getting the bus into the city centre and visit the G.P.O. She would stand in the building and wonder what is was like all those years ago with the bullet's flying and the bomb's exploding and her poor father getting killed.

Her mother Nora was so lonely; she died of a broken heart. She had a strong man who loved her, but he loved Ireland more. Why did her father have to go out and get killed in the bloody rising, and for what? Nobody ever helped her family or recognized her fathers or indeed her families sacrifice. Shot by an English soldier: some innocent young boy. Then she gets pregnant again and Eddie came along, a total accident. That bloody doctor up in the Rotunda hospital wouldn't give her that new tablet, the one to stop a women getting pregnant – bloody pompous old fool. Men! She remembered the night it happened. Him, drunk as usual, stinking of whiskey and tobacco and his corny jokes, forcing himself on her and that stupid grin on his face. A minute or two then he comes like a wild animal. Then he rolls over, farts, and falls asleep snoring like a pig. No, she never wanted Eddie and yet he was a good boy, kind and gentle, so considerate to her. When he used to go to the matinee at the Casino Cinema in Finglas village every Saturday with Paddy he would spent the few pence he got for buying sweets, not on himself, but on buying his mammy a bag of her favourite acid drops which he took home proudly to her. That was her kind son Eddie Kelly. God she loved him so much. He was much more affectionate than Paddy who was somewhat aloof, distant, more like his father.

After Eddie was born she found it difficult to cope with her two young children.

Their flat was situated on the fourth floor of a tenement building opposite Trinity College and accessed by a steep narrow winding timber staircase up which she had to carry all her groceries, pram and her new baby with Paddy clambering behind. But the worst thing was the lack of proper bathroom facilities or hot water. Just one toilet on the landing served the whole building. She hated other peoples' smells.

She applied to Dublin Corporations' Housing Department and a year later was allocated a new three bed roomed two storey house out in Finglas West: a bleak, sprawling estate of small, box-like houses, built out in the country about three miles from the city centre to rehouse families from the inner-city tenements.

Bridie found the new estate cold and isolated with only a few buses a day to and from the city centre. A windswept wasteland far from the hustle and bustle of the city, but at least they had a bathroom, hot water and a small garden. After a while they began to settle in. The boy's made new friends and the memories of their old life in the city slowly began to fade away as the years passed.

Bridie's best friend was Mary O'Toole; one of her neighbours who lived just around the corner. They had something in common: they were both married to men that were unemployed and unemployable. Every Friday night Bridie and Mary would go to bingo in the church hall in the village. On rare occasions

Bridie would be lucky and get a win but she never kept the few pounds for herself. She would give some money to Mary to help her feed and clothe her six children; she needed all the help she could get what with her waster of a husband, the rest she spent buying new clothes for her Eddie. She loved taking Eddie into town to buy him the mod clothes he loved so much. He would pay her back some day, she knew he would. Her little funny cuts Eddie Kelly. This was Bridie's pet name for Eddie. One Saturday she gave Seamy some money to take Eddie for a haircut at the barbers down in the village. When she came back from the shops she found Seamy clumsily trying to cut Eddie's hair with a rusty pair of scissor all to save the few pence for drink. He looked ridiculous sitting with a bowl on his head and Seamy hacking away clumps of hair. Her anger soon turned to laughter at the sight of Eddie's do it yourself haircut. Little funny cuts. It always brought a smile to her face.

She was delighted when Paddy joined the Irish Army and followed in the footsteps of her father. He was gorgeous in his uniform, so tall and handsome. She was so proud of him at his passing out parade at Collin's Barracks. But when the commanding officer shook her hand to congratulate her Seamy butts in and says, "Hey pal, any chance of a feckin gargle around here? I'm bleedin dying of the thirst so I am." She was mortified.

Then out of the blue Paddy gets sent to Africa on some peace-keeping mission. The native tribesmen the Balubas had rebelled against the oppressive Belgian Colonial Government. Bloodshed and massacre followed and the United Nations had stepped in to maintain law and order and protect the civilian population. It was the first time the Irish Army ever served abroad forming part of the United Nation's contingent. Then came the dreadful night the Army messenger came with the news. She saw it all in the dream, that terrible, terrible dream. He was murdered just like her father. Murdering bastards – that's what they were. The Balubas? The English? What's the bloody difference?

Every Sunday afternoon Bridie and Mary O'Toole would walk down the winding Finglas Road and up the steep hill to Glasnevin cemetery to visit Paddy's grave. He was buried at the back of the cemetery, a long way from the main road, beside the Botanic Gardens on a barren piece of ground, isolated from the rest of the cemetery – no fancy grave or headstone, the grave marked by a crooked handmade white painted cross with Paddy's name scrawled in Eddie's spidery handwriting. Eddie had made the makeshift cross out of scraps of wood.

Now and again when she could afford it she would buy fresh flowers for the grave which she lovingly placed beneath the simple wooden cross. On the way out of the graveyard she would always stop for a few minutes and gaze at the plots at the front of the cemetery with the fancy statues and headstones where the famous Irish patriots were interred. And that's where she wanted her eldest son Paddy to be buried. She imagined the beautiful statue, a white marble statue, the finest statue of them all – a statue of Cuchulain the mythical Irish hero, just like the one in the G.P.O. A statue for the dead. She would have 'Paddy Kelly died for Ireland' engraved on the headstone. She would also put an inscription to her father: 'Volunteer Christy Doyle, Irish Citizen's Army, Dublin City Brigade, died for Ireland, Easter 1916'. God, if she could only get her poor father's remains buried with Paddy. Him lying all these years up in an English military graveyard at Arbour Hill and him not even getting a Christian burial; her poor forgotten father. But how in God's name could they ever afford to buy the plot at the front of the cemetery and the marble statue? They hadn't even enough money to feed themselves. Eddie's meagre wages was barely enough to keep them going. She blamed the Government for everything. She remembered the shock of reading the letter. It came from the Department of Defence a couple of weeks after Paddy was killed.

Dear Mr. and Mrs. Kelly,

On behalf of the Government and the Department of Defence we are writing to offer our sincere commiserations with regard to the recent death of your son, Private Patrick Kelly, serial number 9510, 5th Infantry Company, Padraig Pearse Battalion, Eastern Command, killed in action in Katanga, The Congo, Africa while serving in the United Nations peace-keeping force. Unfortunately, it is with great regret that I must inform you on behalf of the Minister that the government is unable to pay you compensation. Regulation 1646 of the Irish Army code states that a minimum amount of twenty percent of the mortal remains of the deceased must be recovered before the government shall be liable to pay compensation or provide a military funeral. Unfortunately, in this instance, the only remains of your son found after he was eaten by the Balubas were his big toe and his half-eaten penis, rendering him ineligible for any monies.

Our deepest sympathy.
Mise le Meas
Stiofan Mac Gillacuddy

She nearly fainted when she read the letter. Cheek of the bastards! Her eldest son gives his life for his country and this is what he gets – nothing. Not even a military funeral or the money to buy a decent grave or a proper headstone. Bastards! Worse than the bloody English. She was never the same after the letter. She went to Doctor Flanagan in the village and he gave her tablets which made her give up and lose all hope.

DANCING WITH CORPSES

Eddie Kelly crossed Parnell's Square and leaving the Friday morning summer sunshine entered the gloomy undertakers. He'd been working for Shaky Shanahan for almost two years now and while he wasn't that fond of the work he enjoyed the company of his employer and, more importantly, he was earning some money to help feed the family now that he was the breadwinner with Paddy gone. In some ways it was better than sitting bored all day having to learn Irish at the Christian Brother's School in Glasnevin.

His father had got him the job. Seamy was barred from his local pub, The Drake Inn, at the top of the hill in Finglas village and one night on the way home from drinking in the Docker's public house he got off the bus at Glasnevin and went to the Gravedigger's pub beside the cemetery. There he met a very drunk Shaky Shanahan who had just buried his life-long undertaker's assistant, Dipper Delaney, earlier that day. Shaky knew Seamy; he was the undertaker for Paddy's funeral, in fact he was sure Seamy still owed him money for the funeral, he just couldn't quite remember. They got talking and Shaky mentioned that he was looking for a new assistant. "Jaysus I've got the very man for yeh Shaky," was Seamy's response. "Sure isn't me very own son Eddie looking for a job now that Paddy gone. I'll bring him down to yeh in the morning so I will."

When Seamy arrived home he rushed up the stairs and into Eddie's bedroom. His son was lying in bed, smoking a cigarette, and listening to a small portable transistor radio his Uncle Sean had sent him from England at Christmas.

"What's dat bleedin shite you're listening to pal?"

Eddie looked at his father, pleasantly surprised at the sudden interest in his music. "It's the House of the Rising Sun, Da," he answered excitedly. "It's The Animals."

"Sound like fuckin animals to me so they do. Shut that bleedin thing off now will yeh and give me head peace. Listen

pal, I've only got two words to say to yeh – *starve the barber.*
Hair cut. Will yeh ever get dat bleedin hair cut, yeh look like a
feckin woman so yeh do. I'm embarrassed just looking at yeh so
I am, I fuckin cringe every time I see dat bleedin hair of yours
so I do."

Seamy hated long hair. One night he tried to cut off Eddie's
hair with the rusty scissors when he was sleeping, but he was
too drunk to hold the scissors. Eddie never got over the shock of
waking up with his father standing over him with a vicious look
on his face, waving a pair of scissor's wildly in the air shouting
"It has to bleedin go, do yeh hear me now pal, it has to bleedin
go". But Eddie refused to get his long hair cut; it was his pride
and joy.

"Anyway pal I've important news for yeh so I have," Seamy
continued. "You're leaving that school of yours tomorrow, I've
got the very job for yeh with Shaky Shanahan as an undertaker's
assistant. We've to go down there tomorrow. It's about time yeh
got yourself a job to help support your ma and me. Things are
very tight now with Paddy going and getting himself killed what
with no compensation or money coming into the house."

The next day Seamy brought Eddie down to Finlater's Place.
Shaky couldn't even recall the previous night's conversation with
Seamy in fact, he remembered very little of the night before, but
he did need a new assistant to help him look after his horse and
wash the corpses now with Dipper gone. At first he didn't think
Eddie was the right one for the job; he seemed too sensitive, too
shy. He just didn't look right. But him and his big mouth again,
always getting him in trouble. He just couldn't say no. So Eddie
Kelly left his school and reluctantly became an undertaker's
assistant. Shaky didn't expect his new employee to last the week
but he did, much to his surprise.

Eddie was a quick learner, handy with Shaky's horse,
Trigger, and good company for Shaky. Although initially scared
of working with the corpses Eddie gradually overcame his
repulsion and became a great help to his new employer.

Shaky greeted Eddie cheerfully, "Morning Eddie me ould
flower, good mornin to yeh son and how are yeh today? Beautiful

day for a funeral so it is, cheer up will yeh, why the glum face Eddie it's Friday, the weekend has landed, sure aren't yeh seeing dat bird of yours tonight, aren't yeh son, what do yeh call her now Colette, dat's it isn't it, Jaysus I always liked the name Colette, very classy name, very classy indeed, yeh know what you're a lucky man Eddie with a bird like dat so yeh are." Shaky continued, "By the way son how's dat father of yours Seamy keeping? Eddie cringed. If Shaky had found out about what his father did with the corpse he might have got the sack.

It was two weeks before and Eddie had been trying to forget about the incident ever since. It happened late on a Thursday afternoon at Glasnevin cemetery when they were undertakers for a poor old spinster from Fatima Mansions; Miss Reilly they called her. She had no relatives or friends and Shaky, Eddie and the priest were the only people at her funeral. After the priest said a few prayers in the small chapel they went to bury the old spinster but when they got to the grave late in the afternoon the gravediggers had gone. They knew that there would be no tip forthcoming what with the old woman being a pauper with no family so they slipped out the back of the cemetery to the nearest pub, leaving Eddie and Shaky with the un-buried corpse.

"Fuck this!" said Shaky. "We'll have to take the old biddy back to the undertakers for the night and try to bury her again in the morning. Eddie come on and I'll buy yeh a pint of Guinness in the Gravediggers and then I'll drive yeh home to Finglas."

They parked the hearse in the small square and entered the bar. The Gravediggers was a quaint old Victorian public house directly adjacent to the cemetery and a regular haunt for funeral parties, undertakers and gravediggers. They found two bar stools, sat down and Shaky ordered a couple of pints of Guinness.

"Yeh know what Eddie, me number one undertaker's assistant; hunger has a thirst so it has and be Jaysus son, I'm about to quench it now so I am. First today." He grabbed the pint, put it to his mouth and drank it down in one hungry gulp, licked his lips, burped and ordered the same again with a double whiskey chaser. Eddie looked on in total astonishment; he hadn't even touched his pint. The two gravediggers who had refused to bury the old spinster sat silently in the corner sipping their pints and cautiously avoiding eye contact with Shaky. Shaky turned to them and said, "Yeh lousy feckers! Fuckin gurriers, dat's what yis are, refusing to bury the poor old spinster, leaving her to lie in her coffin with no proper home to go to."

The gravedigger's remained silent looking sullenly into their pints. After a while Shaky forgot about the gravediggers and got so drunk that he could hardly stand. One of Shaky's undertaker pals, Harry Flower- the freemason, came into the bar and on seeing Shaky's condition insisted on taking him home to his flat in Finlater's Place.

"Jaysus Shaky," he said. "Are yeh drunk again? Yeh know what now you're so fond of the bleedin gargle that you'd drink it off a sore foot so yeh would. You're a fuckin menace and an embarrassment to the undertaker's profession, dat's what yeh are Shaky Shanahan. Now give Eddie the keys of the hearse, you're not fit to drive anywhere so yer not. Here Eddie take the keys and look after the hearse until tomorrow, will yeh son."

Shaky had acquired a new second-hand motor hearse a few weeks before after his horse Trigger was knocked down by a Guinness lorry on the North Wall. It was the driver's fault and the brewery paid Shaky compensation for the loss. With the money Shaky bought a second-hand motor hearse from one of Dublin's big undertakers. Shaky was heartbroken at the death of his beloved animal who had served him well for so many years. "Trigger has to get a decent burial Eddie so she has, after all the long years of faithful service she gave me."

"But Shaky where the hell will we get a coffin big enough for a horse?"

"Don't be thick Eddie we don't need a coffin, we'll just squeeze her into the back of the hearse. It'll be our first burial in the new motor." The dead horse was shoved, with great difficulty, into the back of the hearse, legs sticking out, and driven through the streets of Dublin to the knacker's yard in Ballyfermot much to the hilarity of the general public and adding greatly to Shaky's reputation in the city.

Eddie hadn't got a driving licence but Shaky had let him drive the hearse up and down the lane at the back of the undertakers so he just about knew how to drive. He felt confident enough to take the hearse home and drive it back to Finlater's Place first thing in the morning his house being only a couple of miles up the road from the Gravediggers. He just about managed to negotiate the hearse home and parked it on the footpath. When Bridie saw the hearse with the coffin in the back she said, "Jaysus Eddie, you're not leaving that coffin out in the cold all night. It's disrespectful to the dead. Anyway those thieving bastard's around here are likely to rob it so they are."

Eddie agreed; it was disrespectful to leave the old biddy out in the hearse all night, he also knew Anto O'Toole and his mates would be up drinking all night in the fields behind the estate, sitting around a blazing fire, and when they were drunk they would do anything for a laugh. It was Thursday, unemployment benefit day – cider drinking night. Eddie carried the lightweight coffin into the living room and placed it across the dining room table. *Jaysus*, he thought, *she must be skin and bones, the poor creature. She's as light as a bleedin feather so she is.*

Eddie's father was off on one of his regular drinking binges and hadn't been home for a week. Sometimes his brother Mickey got him casual work on the docks loading and unloading ships. He was paid cash every evening for his work and immediately went to the Dockers where he stayed until closing time. When the bar closed he would stagger over to his brother's tenement flat in Lime Street, sleep on the sofa and be out first thing in the morning, loading potatoes on to the Dublin Packet Steamer's bound for Liverpool on Sir John Rogerson's Quay.

With the coffin laid on the living room table, Eddie and Bridie went to bed but Seamy, who had been drinking all that night in the Dockers, decided on the spur of the moment to get the last bus home to Finglas as the casual work on the ships had ended that evening. Twenty minutes later he got off the bus in the village and staggered towards his house. In his drunken stupor he didn't notice the hearse parked outside the house. He stumbled in the front door and fumbled to find the light switch in the living room. When he switched on the light and to his horror saw a coffin lying on the table.

"Oh sweet Jaysus!" he screamed. "Bridie me darling, your dead." (Bridie was continually complaining about her poor health and how she was always at death's door.) He opened the catches on the cheap flimsy coffin, lifted the lid off, picked up the corpse and started dancing around the living room crying, "Oh Bridie, oh Bridie, forgive me, forgive me, I'll never take a drink again so I won't, what ever happened to you? First me eldest son and now me wife, what in the name of God am I going to do? Bridie you're only skin and bones, me love, me darlin."

On hearing the commotion, Bridie jumped out of her bed and hurried down the stairs. The sight that greeted her almost gave her a heart attack. There was Seamy, in a drunken stupor, waltzing around the living room with the corpse of the old spinster wrapped in a brown pauper's shroud. On seeing Bridie he screamed, "Jaysus, first you take me eldest born son and yeh let him get eaten by dem fuckin Balubas, then you take me darlin wife and now her ghost is here to plague me as well. Holy God what have I ever done to deserve all this?"

Bridie shouted, "Seamy, you dirty feckin eejit. Will yeh ever grow up for Christ's sake? I'm not dead and that's a feckin corpse you're dancing with, would yeh for Christ's sake, put it back in the coffin and have some respect for the dead."

Seamy collapsed on the floor in shock still clutching the corpse. Bridie looked down scornfully at the drunken heap that was her husband. *Christ*, she thought, *how did he ever end up like this?*

"Eddie! Eddie!" she shouted from the bottom of the stairs. No reply. She struggled up the stairs and entered Eddie's bedroom and turned on the light.

"Eddie will yeh ever wake up, for Christ's sake. It's your Da. I need your help son."

Eddie was in a deep sleep, his body sweating profusely and he was muttering incoherently. Bridie shook him hard.

"Eddie wake up for Christ's sake wake up will yeh. It's your Da. I need your help son." Eddie woke up with a startled look in his eyes.

"What's up? What's up, what's the story Ma?"

"Get up quick. I need your help son."

Eddie jumped up quickly, half asleep, and pulled on his trousers. "Jaysus Ma! Yeh woke me out of that dream I've been having, the one I was telling yeh about, the strange dream in the jungle."

"Ah you're just having a nightmare Eddie that's all it was son."

"No Ma. It's not a nightmare. It's a brilliant dream and Ma, there's always a beautiful girl in me dream."

"In your dream's alright," Bridie replied curtly. "In your dreams." Bridie shook her head. Eddie had nightmares ever since Paddys' death about Balubas running up the stairs trying to kill him. She had to laugh. Pity the Balubas didn't come and gobble up that husband of hers only he'd be too tough for the Balubas to eat.

Eddie rushed down the stairs and was shocked at what he saw. "Da! What the fuck do yeh think you're doing? You're not supposed to mess with the corpses so your not. It's not allowed; Shaky will go mad, if he finds out I'll get the sack. You're a menace, Da, a fuckin gobshite, dat's what yeh are, a fuckin gobshite."

Eddie lifted up the corpse and tidied up Miss Reilly. He put her back in the coffin then turned off the living room light and went up the stairs to bed leaving his father lying on the floor sleeping like a child.

Dublin Bay Prawns

Seamy came around at about five o'clock in the morning and stumbled out of the house into the darkness and began walking the three miles or so towards Dublin city centre and the Docker's public house on the quays.

The Dockers was an early house which opened for business at half past six in the morning to cater for workers on night shifts. Just over an hour later, Seamy crossed over Butt Bridge as the first rays of early morning sunshine shimmered gently on the calm waters of the river Liffey. The streets were deserted. Seamy stopped a short distance from the pub and stood staring at the gentle lapping waters below. Then, with the corner of his eye, he spotted the first sign of life. In the shadow's stood a fellow moocher. They nodded without speaking. Then a few minutes later another figure appeared skulking in the shadows. By opening time half a dozen moocher's stood silently and waiting expectantly for the pub to open; shifty darting eyes, greasy hair, scruffy winkle picker boots and smelling of stale tobacco; lost souls who had given up on life and, most of all, on their responsibilities. The bar was their home, safe behind their pints of Guinness and secure in the company of their fellow losers.   Night-time was the moocher's hell; they dreaded having to face their demons. They would toss and turn all night praying for the night to pass and for morning to come. The end of the night never came quickly enough for a moocher. They were all on unemployment benefit, which they seldom gave to their families, and did a little casual work on the side or stole just enough money to keep them going all week in drink and cigarettes and the odd bet on the horses. Forget about the wife and kids; sure, they can look after themselves; sure, wasn't that the women's job? Moocher's were selfish creatures.

Seamy felt better when he saw them; moocher's hated nothing more than their own company. Seamy joined a couple of them outside the pub, anxiously waiting for opening time at half past six, all inhaling deeply on cigarette butts. They nodded to each other without speaking; they didn't have to. When the door finally opened, five minutes later, Seamy rushed in and ordered his first pint of many that day. Moocher's loved a good laugh and he got a lot of mileage out of the corpse story and a few free pints to boot. He was telling the same story at closing time that night.

To everyone who knew him, Seamy Kelly was a good for nothing waster; a drunk, a thief and a complete failure both as a father and a husband. But Seamy hadn't always been like that. When he first saw Bridie on the number ten bus it was love at first sight. She was so beautiful. He saw her every day as she got the bus in to the city to her job as a shop assistant in Cleary's Department Store in O'Connell's Street and coming home again in the evenings. He was smitten. After a few weeks he finally found the courage to ask her out. On their first date he took her to the Theatre Royal in Hawkin's Street to see a show, – Dickie Valentine and the Royalettes. She was so beautiful that night, so slim and elegant. A year later they were married in the Star of the Sea Church in Sandymount. The only one who didn't share their happiness on that beautiful summer's day was Seamy's mother, Patsy. She was broken hearted to be losing her mammy's boy, her youngest son, to Bridie Doyle. Since her husband Michael had died from tuberculosis, when Seamy was very young she doted on him spoilt him rotten. She knew it would all go wrong; no other woman in the world was capable of making her Seamy happy; no other woman was good enough for him. She knew it would all end in tears, many tears for her beloved son.

In the beginning everything was fine for the newlywed couple; they got a small two-roomed flat on the top floor of a rundown tenement building in D'Olier Street which was right in the city centre opposite Trinity College. It suited Seamy well for his work, he could just walk out of the flat and he was on his number ten bus from Trinity College to Sandymount. Then

Bridie became pregnant. They were so happy then, so young, so innocent and in love. During her pregnancy Bridie had a craving for seafood and every night, when Seamy finished his shift, he'd call into the Red Bank fish restaurant opposite their flat and buy Bridie a big bag of Dublin Bay prawns wrapped in newspaper. The young couple would sit on the bare floor of their sparsely furnished flat in front of the gas fire with a pile of big, red, juicy prawn's laid on an open newspaper, laughing and joking under the flickering gas light, while Seamy told his young bride all about the characters he met on his bus run that day. They were so in love then. He was the happiest bus conductor in the city of Dublin.

On the following Saint Patrick's Day their first child was born and Patrick was the name Seamy and Bridie chose for him. Patrick Christopher Kelly. But the arrival of their first child changed everything for Seamy. He couldn't understand why his wife suddenly grew cold and distant. Everything seemed to revolve around their new baby. Bridie just didn't seem to have time for him anymore. For Seamy it was almost as if she had fallen out of love with him. Every night when he got home from work after a hard ten-hour shift, she was in bed with the baby and made him sleep on the couch. This went on for weeks. One night after work he brought her a bag of Dublin Bay prawns but she turned her nose up at his offering and the next morning he found the bag, unopened, in the bin. She wouldn't talk to him anymore, at least not properly. She was shutting him out and he hurt badly.

Instead of rushing home excited each night to see his wife, like he did when they were first married, he started going to Bowes pub in Fleet Street beside their flat and that's where the good-natured Seamy began to lose his self-respect. He began to wither and die inside; a blackness hardening his gentle soul and the pints of Guinness followed by the whiskey chasers helped to dull his sense of loneliness and isolation.

One night he went into the pub after a long day's work with Andy Smyth his bus driver. Andy turned to him and said, "For

Christ's sake Seamy, what the hell is wrong with yeh? You've been like a bag of cats all day the way you were ringing that feckin bell, me back's bleedin killing me so it is with that stop - start stuff. Go easy will yeh. I know something's wrong with yeh, did the wife leave yeh or what?"

"No she came back," Seamy replied sarcastically. He tried to talk to Andy about the situation, but he got short shrift. The only response he got was, "Welcome to the club Seamy me ould flower, welcome to the club. You're now officially a life-long member of the biggest club in Dublin City and by the way yeh don't have to work on the feckin buses to be in this club, everyone's welcome, every class and every creed. Here for Jaysus sake have another pint and a whiskey chaser; that will shut yeh up and will yeh ever stop yer bleedin moaning? Be Jaysus Seamy Kelly you'd give a feckin aspirin a headache so yeh would and for the love of Sweet Jaysus will yeh ever stop ringing the bloody bell so much; if yeh don't stop soon I'll end up in a feckin wheelchair so I will."

When Paddy finally started to sleep in his cot Seamy would come in half-drunk and slip silently into bed beside Bridie desperate for her softness and warmth but all he got was a cold back and silence. He'd lie there in the darkness, listening to the sound of the city traffic, watching the reflection of head lights from cars on the street below move across the ceiling, lonely, isolated and cold, craving for the love and warmth that they once had. He felt so alone and, in desperation. Seamy would sometimes cry for his mother just to hold him and make him feel loved and wanted. He would lie awake all night praying for his wife to turn around and hold him tenderly in the darkness and make everything all right, just like his mother did. But Bridie never ever turned around to give him comfort, to put her arms around him, to hold him close and say, "Seamy, I love you. I love you"

There was no way Bridie Kelly would ever give anything away, no way, especially to her husband. Father Burke had told her that men were just like dogs in heat: only after the one thing; keep them at a distance and give them nothing. And now that she had her beloved son he didn't matter anymore. In total isolation, devoid of love and warmth, Seamy Kelly had two choices: run away to England, meet up with some old pals he knew in London and start a new life; he knew he would get a job easy enough on the buses, look for the love he craved somewhere else, maybe find a young English girl with a cockney accent. The other option was to stay at home and take the easy way out, the Irishman's way – drink: the best cure in the world for all known pain and ailments and especially good for the loneliness. So that's what Seamy decided to do, follow the path of least resistance. Anything to beat the cold back was better than nothing at all.

One Christmas Eve after work, Seamy called into Bowes Pub with Andy Smyth for a few pints of Guinness and a few whiskeys before going home to his flat. One of the regulars in the bar, Dick Cunningham, worked in a jeweller's shop in Grafton Street and got him a beautiful gold bracelet at cost price as a Christmas present for Bridie. He'd worked overtime for months to save the money to be able to afford it. Although he had come to accept his wife's coldness and the lack of love and tenderness in his life, Seamy never stopped loving Bridie. Seamy got home just before midnight, slightly tipsy after six pints of Guinness and four large whiskeys, in good spirits and in a loving mood towards his wife in spite of everything. He was excited as he proudly gave her the gift that he had saved so hard to buy, but she just put it on the mantelpiece without opening it to see what he had given her. The festive season hadn't changed Bridie's coldness towards her husband. No matter what he said or did on that Christmas Eve she was her cold distant self, without love or solace for her husband. When they went to bed after midnight Seamy couldn't control himself any longer. Out of pure desperation and frustration, in a frenzied passion, he forced himself on her. Bridie just lay still her rigid body mocking his animal passion and turned her head away from his breath which stank of whiskey and tobacco.

Seamy sensed her total apathy. She lay beneath him cold and unmoving.

In animal desperation he climaxed, and on the cold bed of their marriage, without any tenderness or love in the early hours of a Christmas morning in 1950 as soft snowflake's fell gently over the city of Dublin, Eddie Kelly was conceived – the product of six pints of Guinness, four double Jameson whiskeys and his father's animal frustration.

That night was the end for Seamy; he just gave up on Bridie, his marriage and most of all on himself. She didn't respect him; she didn't love him anymore. He went sour inside and lost his good humour; he never again shared the marital bed with his wife. He drank more and more and was finally sacked for stealing bus fares to buy even more drink.

LOSING THE O

They had only one corpse that day and no burials and as Eddie washed down the shrunken figure of a one-legged old man he couldn't help but think about the corpse lying on the slab. He often wondered about the dead people.

Shaky read his thoughts. "Dat fella," he said pointing at the shrunken that figure Eddie was washing. "He had a hard life, Eddie, so he had. Name of Joe Cassidy; he was a docker till he got hurt in the Great Lock Out in 13; lost a leg, so he did the poor creature. The working people were starving and they had to fight back against the bosses. The police were brutal, so they were. It was terrible Eddie, yis young ones could never understand the suffering those poor people went through to give yis everything yis have today."

Everything we have today? Eddie thought.

"One of Jim Larkin's union men so he was. Wasn't your grandfather one of Jim Larkin's union men, Eddie? Didn't he come out with the Citizen's Army under big Jem Connolly in the 16 rebellion?"

Eddie didn't reply and Shaky continued. "Yeh know what, Eddie? I think that your grandfather might have fought with the wrong crowd in the rising."

Eddie looked hard at Shaky. "What the fuck do yeh mean by dat Shaky? Yeh mean dat he should have fought with the English?"

Shaky saw the hurt and anger in Eddie's reddening face. "No son no, you've got me all wrong. I mean Pearse's lot, the republicans; they won the war in the end not Jem Connolly and the workers. All we did was swap one feckin flag for another. What was the point of it all? We never got the worker's republic, did we now? The poor are still poor and all the young people having to emigrate to find work – it's our best export. The scourge of the country, so it is – a terrible scourge." Shaky knew he'd said the wrong thing again; him and his big mouth. He quickly changed the subject. "Anyway, Eddie, as I was saying, dat fella your washing, yeh your man there; a tram wheel took his leg off, back in 13 in the Great Lockout. He was blocking the road down at Bachelor's Walk, trying to stop the scab drivers so he was, and dat's how he got hurt. Dirty bastard drove over him, took his leg off from the knee. Wasn't your grandfather a tram driver son?"

Eddie didn't answer.

Shaky continued. "Hard life the poor creature had. Anyway, it's all over now, at least for him, so it is. Dead fellas don't have a care in the world Eddie, well not in this world anyway; I can't say anything about the next. Yeh can't send a dead fella a bill; do yeh know dat son? So maybe he's better off now."

"Jaysus!" replied Eddie looking at Shaky, a slight anger in his voice. "You're smart, so feckin smart, so yeh are. What's the use in living if you're better off dead? Where's the sense in dat Shaky for fuck's sake? What's the point in being alive if you're better off dead? Answer me that one if yeh can."

Shaky turned to Eddie with a serious look on his face. "Look son, we all have to die some time and dat's a dead cert, pardon the pun; that's the easy bit so it is, but here's the hard bit. Yeh can't just press a button and die when you want to son so yeh can't. Do yeh understand me now Eddie? Nobody knows when they're going to die."

Eddie looked at Shaky puzzled at what he was saying.

"Do yeh not get my point son? Eddie look; see that poor fella lying there all stiff and cold, now he's gone for the milk alright so he has. When he lost his leg he couldn't get work. How could he? He was a docker. His life was as good as over but he couldn't just end it there and then; he couldn't just lie down and die so he had to go on living with all the pain and misery and him with a wife and seven kids to feed. Ended up the rest of his life on O'Connell's Street selling newspapers so he did. Hop Along; yeh dat's what they called him – Hop Along Cassidy. Do yeh get it, Eddie? Hop Along Cassidy?" Shaky laughed. "Now son, dat's the real tragedy of life, the living bit with all the misery, the heartbreak and disappointment; the dying bit's the easy bit.

Anyone can die. It's easy so it is. It's the living bit dat's hard so it is Eddie, not the dying bit. We can't just turn off all the pain and suffering when we want to, unless you top yourself of course. Dat's no good is it son, dat's a mortal sin so it is; eternal damnation for the soul, cast into hell with the devil for company; worse than being alive with all the disappointment and the pain and the misery and to make it worse Eddie they say the devil's an Englishman so they do. Can yeh imagine dat Eddie? A fate worse than death." Shaky laughed again. "Yeh, Eddie a fate worse than bloody death."

What the fuck is he talking about? Eddie thought. *Jaysus, Shakys a queer fella at times, very deep, deep as the ocean, so he is. Comes out with some very strange things does old Shaky Shanahan.*

Anyway enough talk about all the misery and dying stuff; it was Friday and Friday night was Eddie's big night out. Eddie lived for his Friday nights. He would get home from work, wash; get dressed in his best mod clothes and head down to the city centre to his favourite pub the Ace of Spades.

The Ace of Spades was an old Victorian public house on the quays of the river Liffey, near the docks and close to the city centre. It was a typical old-fashioned Dublin public house with sawdust on the wooden floor, dark wood panelling on the walls and the ceiling height polished mirrors behind the bar. A big grandfather clock hung on the wall behind the bar with the tick-tock of the swinging pendulum slowly marking away the time. He would sit on his favourite bar stool at the back of the bar until closing time drinking pint after pint of Guinness, puffing away on his Woodbine cigarettes and slipping into a lovely sense of well-being. He would feel remote, distant from all his problems. It was the one night he could forget about his ma and almost forget about Paddy. He could put all the dying and suffering stuff to the back of his mind, even if it was for only one night.

Eddie loved that Friday night feeling, getting drunk, disappearing into a world of his own and dreaming about what exciting things might happen. Eddie had many friends but he didn't like to meet them first thing on his Friday night out. He preferred to go into the city early and sit alone all night on his bar stool enjoying his own company and looking at his reflection in the dark tinted mirror behind the bar; his friends only interrupting the private world of his thoughts. Their company irritated him. He loved to daydream about what exciting things might happen on his Friday night out; maybe he might get lucky with Colette Murphy and she'd let him go all the way or even get a feel.

After the pub closed Eddie would walk the short distance to the Go-Go beat club in Abbey Street. In the small, sweaty basement club, the drunken crowd would dance the night away to the pulsating music. It was Eddie's idea of heaven on earth and for a few hours it *was* Eddie's heaven on earth, but he yearned for a bit more excitement in his dull life.

Some of Eddie's friends had moved to London after leaving Saint Vincent's Christian Brother School in Glasnevin. When they came home to Dublin at Christmas or at holiday times they would tell him all about exciting London, the hippies, Brick Lane and all the other exciting places. He had often thought seriously about moving over to London but he was going nowhere. He couldn't go anywhere. He had to stay home and look after his ma and da and keep the house going. Without his wages they would starve to death. It all went wrong when Paddy died; Paddy's death changed everything. *Jaysus* Eddie thought *why did the Balubas have to kill me big brother? He had to go and get feckin eaten by the Balubas thousands of miles away on the far side of the world in Africa and his ma going on and on all the time about her bloody fancy grave and a marble statue for Paddy. He knew she'd gone funny in the head since Paddy was killed; nothing else mattered to her except the fancy grave and the big statue. How could they ever afford a fancy grave and a marble statue when they had barely enough to eat? If pigs could fly?*

"Eddie! Eddie!" Shaky shouted, interrupting Eddie's deep thoughts. "Son," he continued a serious tone in his voice. "Did

I ever tell you that me name used to be Shaky O'Shanahan not just plain Shaky Shanahan?"

"So bleedin what?" replied Eddie. "Who gives a fuck?"

"No," said Shaky, "I'm not joking, Eddie. Me name used to be Shaky O'Shanahan. Do you understand what I'm saying now son?"

"No," replied Eddie. "But you're going to tell me anyway aren't yeh, fire away."

"Well it was like this," said Shaky seriously, "one night I was in Mulligan's pub and, would you ever believe it Eddie? I got as drunk as hell and when I got home me name wasn't Shaky O'Shanahan anymore. Jaysus would you ever believe it Eddie? I was just poor old Shaky Shanahan." Shaky turned away.

Eddie was curious. "What happened, Shaky?"

"I lost the O in me name," replied Shaky.

Eddie looked puzzled. "What do yeh mean yeh lost the O in your name? Jaysus Shaky, how the feck could yeh lose the O in your name? Dat's something else Shaky so it is."

"I think I must have lost it in the toilets of Mulligan's pub and I never found it to this very day. Would you ever believe dat? Isn't that terrible Eddie? I goes into the toilets in Mulligan's pub drunk and whatever happens when I come out I'd lost the O in me name. I'd become plain old Shaky Shanahan."

Eddie stared blankly at Shaky. Was that a joke or was dat for real? He wasn't sure. *Jaysus*, he thought *that Shaky Shanahan's not the full shilling so he's not.* But was there some truth in what Shaky was saying. Shaky's father was a hardworking thrifty man and a teetotaller. Shaky Shanahan was born in the Liberties area of Dublin City in 1902. His mother died bringing her only child into the world. His father worked hard and built up his undertaker's business and was able to buy a large Georgian building in Finlater's Place, moving to a better part of the city and running his business from a large outhouse at the rear of the premises. At twelve years of age Shaky became his father's assistant and learned the art of undertaking. His father was very strict and when Shaky was older he wasn't allowed to drink nor have girlfriends. When his father died suddenly from a heart attack Shaky became the sole proprietor. However his father's death had a very bad effect on Shaky – he lost all control. He began to drink, spending all his money in the bars of Dublin. The building at Finlater's Place fell into disrepair and after the collapse of an old Georgian tenement building in close proximity to Shaky's premises the Corporation issued a notice to Shaky requiring him to carry out major structural repairs which he could not afford.

Drunk one night, he sold the building to the auctioneer Lexie White from the North Circular Road for a pittance, keeping only the outhouse to the rear for his business. In a short time spending the little money he'd got for the building on drink. Without realising it Shaky was not joking about his name. As O is a patronymic for 'son of', Shaky did indeed lose the O in his name in the toilets of every public house in the city Dublin, Mulligans being only one of many where Shaky pissed away his birthright while drowning his honour in the shallow cup and selling his reputation for a song.

G Men

After work Eddie stood on the crowded bus on his way home to Finglas West with his week's wages, a crisp twenty-pound, held tightly in his hand. He felt like the richest man in the world. As the bus trundled slowly past Glasnevin Cemetery he imagined for a second that he could see the statue – A big, white, shiny marble statue of Cuchulain right at the front of the cemetery. He could see the inscription on the statue – *Paddy Kelly died for Ireland*. They would leave out the *'eaten by Balubas'* bit; it just didn't sound right. But that would never ever happen. Where the hell would they get the money for an expensive grave and a fancy marble statue?

When he got off the bus Eddie went to Moroney's fish and chip shop in the village and bought three one and one's – ray and chips for himself and his ma and da. Friday night was fish and chip night. When he arrived home he ate his dinner in silence. After dinner, he went to the bathroom, undressed, half-filled the bath with cold water, stepped in and scrubbed his body hard all over with carbolic soap to remove any taint of the dead bodies from his skin. Then he doused himself in Old Spice after shave lotion, a Christmas present from Colette Murphy, and dressed in his new mod clothes which his mother had bought for him in Arnott's Department Store a couple of weeks before, out of her bingo winnings – flared trousers, leather brogue shoes, a collarless granddad shirt and a Fair Isle jumper. He looked at himself in the small cracked mirror as he combed his long hair. He looked good and smelled good.

As he left his bedroom and walked towards the stairs Eddie stopped suddenly as he passed the half-open door. It was his brother Paddy's old bedroom – Private Paddy Christopher Kelly, 5th Infantry Company, Padraig Pearse Battalion, Eastern Command, Irish Defence Forces. He slowly pushed open the bedroom door. The room was ice cold and had a musty smell like the funeral parlour. The curtains were drawn and the soft flickering red light of the Sacred Heart lamp over the fireplace cast an eerie glow on the walls and ceiling of the darkened room. Nothing had been touched in the room since Paddy's death; a green Irish Army uniform lay neatly folded on the bed, shiny medals pinned on the chest. On the walls were Paddy's posters of Elvis Presley and a faded black and white photograph of the U.S. president John F.Kennedy, on a visit to Ireland a few years previous. Paddy's silver Erin's Isle Gaelic football medals lay neatly on the dresser and an old German Mauser pistol lay on the bed beside the uniform. The pistol had belonged to Eddie's grandfather, Christy Doyle, and had been smuggled in on the Liverpool boat by a sailor. It was one of the first guns in the hands of the Dublin Citizen's Army.

Eddie walked over to the bed and lifted the old German pistol. It felt heavy. How many people had it killed Eddie wondered as he looked down at the gun that he now held in his hand? He knew it had killed someone; his mother had told him. His grandfather had killed a man with this very gun. It was Matt Corrigan one of Christy Doyle's comrades in the trade union movement. Corrigan was a postman but also a volunteer in the Citizen's Army. He used his job well gathering information on the homes of Dublin Metropolitan policemen and Government officials. But the English were suspicious of Corrigan and in the early hours of the morning he was arrested by the G Men at his house in Irishtown and taken to the notorious interrogation room at Dublin Castle. The G Men were members of an elite squad of Irish special branch officer's working directly for the Government intelligence services. Corrigan didn't last long. In the dark, dank interrogation room he was hung on a meat hook and beaten to a pulp, his face so badly disfigured that he was no longer recognisable, his hanging figure casting a ghostly shadow on the blood-splattered white-washed walls of the interrogation room. He refused to betray his comrades. He would rather die. He closed his eyes and prayed to his maker – let the end be quick. But he wasn't to die that night. Major Morley had stood in the shadows watching the G Men do what they did best. When

Corrigan began to lose consciousness Morley stepped forward. "Enough," he shouted. "I don't want the Fenian bastard dead, at least not yet. Let him down."

Corrigan collapsed in a crumpled heap on the cold stone floor. Morley knelt down beside him and grabbed his blood-matted hair. "Listen now postman you're not going to die, at least not now, you Fenian bastard. I want information you know things. You know names; names that I want to know."

With his last ounce of energy, Corrigan half-opened his bloody eyes, focused on Morley and spat blood and broken teeth into his face. Morley jumped up quickly wiping himself with a handkerchief.

"Corrigan you have a son don't you now. What's his name? Yes John that's it now isn't it? If you don't tell me what I want to know I'll kill your son. I'll have the G Men bring him here right now, tonight, so he can see his beloved father then I'll hang him in front of you."

Corrigan knew Morley was serious, this was no idle threat. He knew what Morley was capable of; he'd seen his bloody work all over the city. He looked up at the major: the bastard in his fancy officer's uniform with the twisted smile on his moustached face – 'The hoof of the horse, the horn of the bull and the smile of the Englishman.' Then he told Major Morley all he wanted to know. He had no choice; he knew Morley would kill his young son. When he had told them enough he was thrown in the back of a lorry and his broken body dumped on a deserted street near his home in Irishtown. He wanted to run, to hide away, but where could he go? He crawled home; he knew his fate was sealed. He knew he was a dead man walking or, in his case, a dead man crawling. After several Citizens' Army Volunteers were arrested the next day by the G Men word soon got out about Corrigan's arrest. They knew he had informed. An informer's fate was death. They drew straws to decide who would be the executioner. Christy Doyle drew the short straw and became the assassin, shooting his comrade twice in the head at point blank range as his wife and son looked on.

Christ! No wonder we have so much bad luck in this family,
Eddie thought, what with his grandfather killing the postman.
It was cold-blooded murder. Maybe they were cursed; that
would explain a lot of things. Maybe the postman had cursed
them. He shuddered and dropped the gun on the bed. He gently
touched the uniform and felt the cold metal of Paddy's shiny
service medals, he could still smell Paddy: a faint smell of cheap
hair oil and stale tobacco. Christ he missed Paddy so much, why
did he have to go and get eaten by the Balubas in Africa. He
turned quickly and left the room.

Enough of the sadness and memories, he was going out to the
pub, his special place – the Ace of Spades. He was going to ride
the high stool and leave the sad memories at home, at least for
the time being. Eddie rushed out of the house without saying
goodbye to his parents ran down to the village and caught the
number forty bus to the city centre and his favourite watering
hole.

DUBLIN TALK

Eddie walked cheerfully with a bounce in his step along the quays towards his favourite pub. He felt good. It was a beautiful July evening in Dublin, the soft sunlight reflecting on the calm waters of the river Liffey, the beautiful summer evening reflecting Eddie's good mood. As he pushed open the door of the noisy crowded bar a warm gush of beer-smelling air hit him in the face. He felt a tingle of excitement and anticipation. He felt intoxicated and he hadn't even had a pint. He settled on his favourite bar stool at the gloomy end of the pub and called to the barman. "Hey Terry how yeh doing pal? A pint of your best Guinness please and give us a plate of your lovely cheese with plenty of mustard." He liked the pungent taste of the English mustard on strong cheddar cheese washed down with a pint of Guinness. Eddie was still hungry; he always had a hungry feeling, never quite full. "And how is my favourite undertaker's assistant Mister Kelly tonight?" asked the barman. "Man on a mission Terry," Eddie replied, licking his lips in anticipation of the tall, black, cool pint of Guinness settling at the taps all for him.

He glanced around the crowded bar. As usual the bar was packed with groups of old men huddled around tables laughing and joking. The darkness of the pub was only interrupted when someone entered and for a second or two shafts of brilliant sunlight penetrated the dark recesses of the smoke-filled bar room like a bright spotlight illuminating the swirling dancing smoke particles and the odd perfect smoke halo rising heavenward.

"There yeh go," said the barman placing a pint of Guinness, all shiny and black with a creamy head, on the shiny bar counter beside a large plate of neatly sliced cheddar cheese with a big dollop of English mustard. As he supped his pint and devoured the cheese and mustard he began to think about his girlfriend Colette Murphy. Colette worked as a shop assistant in Woolworths in Henry Street and still lived in the city centre. She was Eddie's first and only girlfriend and the first girl he had ever kissed. But she was playing hard to get, very hard to get. She wanted a steady relationship with someone who would settle down, get married and have children, but Eddie had no such ideas. He met Colette in the Go-Go club every Friday night. When the Go-Go club finished he would always walk her home to her flat in Sheriff Street. He always tried it on with her without any luck. She was keeping herself until she was married and any funny business was totally out of the question much to Eddie's frustration. Occasionally he might be lucky and she might let him touch her breasts and if he was very lucky she'd touch him through his trousers and get him aroused but he never gave up and any chance he got he tried it on with her. He did love her in a funny sort of way but love wasn't exactly what he had on his mind especially when he was drunk on a Friday night. Eddie felt good as he sat at the bar supping on his Guinness, he wasn't exactly sure why; maybe it was something to do with the beautiful summer evening outside. He felt that something exciting might happen that night. He finished his first pint quickly and ordered another round. Every now and then someone passing Eddie on the way to the toilets would make a joke about undertakers. "And how's young Kelly tonight? I believe there's stiff competition in your line of work." It never stopped the same old boring jokes.

As the night wore on the pints of Guinness began to have the desired effect and he felt the warm glow of alcohol from his head to his toes.

He looked at his reflection in the mirror behind the bar – long brown hair and round wire spectacles he bought for a shilling at the Dandelion market up beside Stephen's Green; the Fair Isle jumper looked good with the collarless granddad shirt. The salesman in Arnott's had looked at Eddie in disbelief when he discarded the detachable collars that came with it.

"It's the new mod style," Eddie said to the surprised salesman.

Shaky Shanahan said that he looked a bit liked that dirty old queer fella, James Joyce, from up Cabra way, but who the fuck was James Joyce?

Eddie noticed that as he got drunk everything around him seemed different, slightly blurred, gently out of focus. But what he noticed most of all was the sound. He was in a packed, noisy bar room full of old men drinking Guinness and chattering away. One minute they were really loud and the next minute the noise dropped to a soft distant whisper. When he wanted to he could listen intently and hear every word that was said in their conversation and then slowly the conversation would drift away into the distance, almost to a whisper. The sound reminded Eddie of the waves coming and going on Sandymount strand, in out, in out. He noticed how the men in the bar talked round and round in circles. This was Dublin talk. Eddie listened intently to a particular group of old men chattering away in the corner near where he was sitting. They were having a deep conversation about the cost of living in Dublin and the high taxation on the price of a pint of Guinness when one old man interrupted the flow of conversation and suddenly shouted. "It was dem Viking fellas dat's who it was. It was dem Viking fellas. They became as Irish as the Irish themselves, yeh dat's what dem fellas did; they became as Irish as the Irish themselves."

The old men listened intently as he continued. "They sailed past this very pub in their big boats, so they did, coming up the Liffey." He pointed towards the river and all the old men looked in that direction. "Yeh wouldn't have caught dem fellas coming in here for a pint, no way, not with the feckin tax we have to pay. If they'd known about the tax in the first place they'd never have come to Ireland, no bleedin way."

As the bar door swung open for a second Eddie looked out at the river Liffey and imagined a long Viking ship full of wild-looking hairy men, swords and axes in hand, all staring desperately at the bar, tongues hanging out and them all dying of the thirst having just rowed all the way from Viking land, where ever the fuck Viking land was. The conversation rambled on and on and Eddie suddenly noticed that they were talking about him. He felt uncomfortable. His face reddened. He resented anyone invading his private space, his special world. He felt exposed, vulnerable.

"See him over there?" an old man pointed his bony finger at Eddie. "See him with the long hair? Yeh, dat fella dat looks like a feckin woman; isn't he from Finglas? Isn't his father dat alcoholic fella? What do yeh call him now? Yeh, Seamy, dat's it – Seamy Kelly from Ringsend, got sacked off the buses for robbin bus fares, so he did. Doesn't your man there, doesn't he work for dat ould eejit, Shaky Shanahan?"

"Yeh, he's an undertaker's assistant." Another man joined the conversion. "Wasn't it his brother dat was eatin by the blackies out in Africa? What do yeh call dem now? Balubas, dat's it, Balubas. Didn't they eat him up just like pigs' feet? The greedy fuckers. In the army so he was. Dem black fellas, they'd eat anything so they would. Dirt birds, dat's what they are, fuckin dirt birds. Jaysus dem blackies," he continued, "Yeh couldn't trust dem black fellas as far as yeh could throw dem; stab yeh in the back so they would, dem black fellas, yeh with their spears." They all laughed.

"Yeh," he continued. "Even dem English had trouble with the black fellas. Now, if the long fella, big Mick Collins, if he was here, he'd have sorted dem out all right.

Yeh the long fella he'd a given dem blackies the rub of the feckin relic so he would." The old man continued, "Yeh I knew Michael Collins well so I did sure didn't I fight beside him in the G.P.O. Comrades in arms so we were? I remember the 16 rising like it was yesterday. Sure wasn't I there in the front row, didn't I shoot a hundred of the Tommies me very own self so I did; gunned dem down like dogs.

Here we go again, Eddie thought. Every fecker in Dublin was in the 1916 rising. Christ it must have been a full house, they must have been queuing up all night to get into the G. P.O. He could see it all now: Padraig Pearse in his fancy new tailor-made uniform straight from Saville Row in London, a green feather in his hat, holding a shiny new Wilkinson's silver sword standing beside James Connolly dressed in his cheap handmade uniform and holding an old rusty second-hand gun. He even saw his grandfather, Christy Doyle, standing beside James Connolly at the front door of the G.P.O. in his Citizen's Army uniform collecting the entrance tickets, Pearse shouting, "Come on folks, come on now. Get your bullets; get your bullets here for the Easter Rising. Come on folks, come on. Get your bullets here, five for a pound, five for a pound. Shoot to kill, shoot to kill. Come on now folks, get your bullets here. Shoot an English soldier for Ireland."

Jaysus, Eddie thought, *they must have come from all over the country to get into the G.P.O., them coming by the thousands by train and by the bus load. It must have been a packed house in 1916 – standing room only, packed in like bleedin sardines. Christ what a load of bollocks. If they hadn't put the English out of Dublin we wouldn't have this boring kip now. We should apologise to the English and ask them to come back as long as they bring all those lovely birds in the miniskirts and the music; it would be fantastic. This kip is full of nuthin except all that show band rubbish: Dickie fuckin Dock, Georgie fucking Porgie – did you ever hear such shite in all your life? Dickie fucking cock more like it, ugly bastard too; face like a fuckin burnt banana.*

Eddie loved rock music and not the show band music that prevailed in Dublin. Every night Eddie would tune into Radio Luxemburg on his transistor radio, listen to all the English chart hits and practice dancing to the music all to impress Colette Murphy in the Go-Go club on a Friday night. He loved rock and pop music and the top ten hits but he hated the Irish country and western music played by the show bands. That's what Eddie loved most about the Go-Go club; sometimes they had great blues' bands down from Belfast – Moses K and the Prophets, The Taste, brilliant; dancing all night in the packed basement club, sweating bodies and sweating walls – massive. Look out girls here I come.

As he sat on the bar stool he began to think about the night ahead. *Maybe tonight would be his lucky night, tonight did feel sort of special, different than usual a bit of a buzz in the air.*

Yeh, he thought, *maybe tonight's the night me boat will come in. Please God let me boat come in tonight. Maybe Colette will come good and let me go all the way.*

He began to feel aroused. His whole body quivered with excitement. His heart raced. *Jaysus,* he thought, *stop the lights. Down boy down; I'm starting to get the bleedin horn thinking about Colette Murphy so I am.*

BLACK FACES

At the same time that Eddie Kelly sat in the Ace of Spades public house, smiling at his own reflection in the mirror behind the bar, a young black sailor called Jerome King walked briskly down the gang plank of the United States warship, the USS Neptune, out of Virginia and stepped on to dry land for the first time in more than four weeks. The warship had docked in Dublin earlier that evening.

A group of sailor's piled into two waiting taxis to take them the mile or so to the city centre for a night of drink and women, their first drink since the States. One of the sailors called to Jerome, "Come on get in buddy, we're hitting the town."

"No brother you go on." Jerome replied. "I want to walk to the city and take in the sights, you go on and I'll catch you guys later."

As the taxis drove off towards the city centre Jerome turned to the sailor on watch duty who was his best friend and said, "See yah later Sonny keep it cool brother."

Sonny nodded in reply. *That's one strange dude,* he thought. *A bit of a loner is that brother.*

Sonny and Jerome were from the same neighbourhood in Detroit and had spent some time in police custody together and were good friends. By chance they ended up together in the navy and serving on the Neptune.

As Jerome walked along the deserted quays of the Dublin docks in the warm evening sunshine he was surprised at the strangeness of the place, the smallness of everything and the pervading smell. What was that smell? This was the first time he had been in Europe, first time in a foreign country, his first time away from the States and everything looked so small and run down, so old and neglected. There was a sense of emptiness about the place, a sort of sadness; he couldn't quite figure it out; it sort of gave him the creeps. And the place was deserted; not a soul in sight, the stillness of the summer's evening only interrupted by the occasional cries of seagull's overhead. When he thought about his folks back home he felt slightly homesick. He missed his young brothers and sisters, his father and most of all his mum's cooking. But he thought to himself, *what the heck. I'm seeing the world and getting well paid by Uncles Sam's navy and able to send home plenty of dollar's every month to help my family and they sure need help. Better than three long years in the state penitentiary.*

Jerome had been lucky. He was expelled from school and had got involved in a neighbourhood gang in the projects and was arrested for possession of drugs. It broke his parent's hearts. His mum and pop were old-fashioned, deeply religious folk from Louisiana that had moved to Detroit where Jerome's father found work in the Ford motor plant. They were a poor family and Jerome's father found it hard to support his children. In desperation, after his arrest, Jerome's parents went to the minister of their church for help, to act as a character witness for their son at his trial. The minister pleaded with the judge for clemency on Jerome's behalf and the judge gave him the choice of three years in the state penitentiary or three years service in the army or navy. Jerome chose the navy as the best option and six months later here he was in Dublin, Ireland, Europe, dressed in a smart sailor's uniform with money in his pocket.

He knew very little about Ireland except what a cook on the Neptune, whose folks were American Irish, had told him. O'Brien had said it was all green, full of lakes, mountains and cottages but as he looked around all he could see were deserted docks and rundown buildings – dingy, smelly with not a mountain or cottage in sight.

Jerome had refused to join his buddies in the taxi because he wanted to enjoy the experience of this strange place for himself. His buddies would only distract him. All they wanted to do was get drunk and pick up some local girls He wanted something different.

After a short walk along the quays he passed the Custom House and, as he approached the city, he began to see the first signs of life, an old man walking a dog who looked at him strangely. Then, as he neared the city centre he passed a young couple walking hand in hand laughing and joking. He noticed how they stopped laughing when they saw him and just stared – *must be the uniform.*

As he walked briskly along the quays he passed a public house. The door of the bar suddenly swung open and Jerome, for a split second, caught a glimpse of a dimly lit, smoky bar room packed with dark figures huddled around tables drinking and chatting. But it was the smell of beer and the sudden burst of noise that caught his attention. He was fascinated by the noise and the smell; nothing like the bars back home in the States. The place was so old fashioned. It reminded him of the saloon bars in the cowboy films: long, wooden bar counter; sawdust on the floor; dark, smoky and very inviting; a man's bar. Without thinking twice he left the bright evening sunshine and entered the long, dark, bar room. It took a few seconds for his eyes to focus in the smoke-filled room.

The bar was full of old men huddled around tables who suddenly stopped talking and looked at him with astonishment. Most of them had never seen a black face before. He walked down the crowded room to find a space at the bar to order a drink.

As he reached the end of the long bar he saw a young guy, a hippie with long hair, sitting by himself, somewhat distant from the rest of the drinkers and smiling at his reflection in the mirror behind the bar. The young hippie looked totally out of place amongst all the old men, in a world of his own, totally detached. For some reason Jerome suddenly felt at ease and was drawn towards the solitary figure. He was the youngest person in the bar and stood out from the rest of the customers just like himself. As Jerome came up behind Eddie he noticed that the hippie guy seemed totally spaced out with a self satisfying expression on his face.

Maybe this guy is on drugs or something, thought Jerome. *I'd like to try his shit.*

As Eddie smiled to himself in the mirror behind the bar he thought about the prospect of going the whole way with Colette Murphy later that night; his heart raced and his body trembling

45

with anticipation and excitement. In the mirror everything around him looked distant and hazy except his image; he looked crystal clear, really buzzing. Suddenly something began to focus behind his own reflection in the mirror.

What the fuck? No, it couldn't be.

He took a long swig out of his drink and shook his head to refocus. He looked again. Christ, it was still there; staring over his shoulder was a black face. *Jaysus*, he thought, *the Balubas have come to get me just like they got Paddy.* This had been his worst nightmare for years, the Balubas coming to get him.

For a year after Paddy was killed Eddie had nightmares every night about the Balubas, hordes of half-naked Balubas, with their knives and spears running after him around Finglas village and chasing up the stairs of his house trying to kill him and eat him just like poor Paddy. He would run into Paddy's bedroom and grab the Mauser pistol and aim it at the Baluba with the wild eyes who was about to stab him. He would pull the trigger but nothing would happen; the gun was useless. He was dead. It was all over.

No it couldn't be. Christ I must be drunk.

He took another quick gulp from his pint, closed his eyes for a second and looked again in the mirror. The Baluba was still standing there larger than life smiling at him. He must be dreaming. He turned around slowly and, to his utter amazement, stood a tall, lean, black man with a friendly face dressed in a sailor's uniform.

Jaysus a fuckin sailor from the docks. Thank God for dat.

"Hey Terry," shouted Eddie. "Give this sailor fella a pint of the black stuff will yeh. I'm buying." Eddie's over-friendliness was a direct reaction to the relief that his worst nightmare had not come true and that the Balubas had not come to get him.

"How yah doing buddy?" said the black sailor holding out his hand to Eddie. "Name's Jerome," he continued, "just docked in Dublin this evening on the warship USS Neptune out of Norfolk, Virginia. Sailing on a twelve-month tour of duty, first time in Ireland."

"Glad to meet you Jerome," replied the relieved Eddie warmly. "Eddie Kelly's the name; undertaker's assistant, welcome to Dublin."

"Here," said Eddie, pulling over a bar stool. "Park your arse there, pal." Eddie handed the young sailor a Woodbine cigarette. "Here pal have a cancer stick."

"There yeh go," said the barman handing Jerome a creamy pint of Guinness. Terry caught the look of surprise on the young sailor's face when he saw the black colour of the Guinness. "Goes well with your complexion pal," Terry said laughing.

"Say Eddie," asked Jerome, "what kind of drink is this? I've never seen a beer like this before." He was amazed – a black beer; 'The black stuff'.

"Err, no offence pal," replied Eddie smiling. "Just look around yeh, some of dem old fellas over there – they're all over a hundred years old – all they do all day long is drink the black stuff; live forever dem fellas will."

Jerome smiled. He liked the Dublin humour and easy relaxed way of the young Irish lad. O'Brien on the ship had said the Irish were very friendly and loved a good laugh and he could see what he'd meant.

Eddie had never met an American before, let alone a black one, and he really enjoyed the young sailor's company. Jerome told Eddie all about the States and the black soul music. The sailor fascinated Eddie and he didn't mind that Jerome had interrupted his normal Friday night; he was glad to spend the evening with the young sailor, someone new and different to talk to. Every now and then one of the old men would buy Jerome a pint and sit down for a chat curious to meet the sailor and hear about life in the American Navy. Jerome felt at ease with Eddie and was fascinated with the Dublin conversation although he could hardly understand a word they said.

The night wore on and many pints of Guinness were drunk. Eddie told the sailor all about his job as an undertaker's assistant and about Shaky Shanahan and before they knew it, it was closing time. "Time now, gentlemen, time now please. Have yis no homes to go to? Time now gentlemen time, please." Terry began ringing the bar bell incessantly.

They finished their drinks and reluctantly left the warm cosy atmosphere of the crowded bar and Eddie invited his new friend Jerome to come over to go to the Go-Go club with him to meet all his mates and Colette Murphy. "You might even pull a bird," said Eddie to Jerome. "The Dublin birds all love a fella in a uniform." He smiled briefly as he thought for a second about Paddy and how all the girls in Finglas village would shout at him when he walked up the hill in the village dressed in his army uniform. *"Go on yeh good thing."* All the girl's loved Paddy. "But," Eddie continued, "I have to warn yeh; yeh have as much chance of getting a feckin ride off a nun as yeh have off a Dublin bird. They're all saving themselves till they're married pal and I'll tell yeh something for nuthin, I should bleedin know so I should" Jerome smiled. He hadn't a clue what Eddie meant but he was honoured that his new friend had invited him to join him on his night out at the Go-Go club.

SHIPS IN THE NIGHT

They left the Ace of Spades public house and walked briskly down O'Connell's Street towards the Go-Go club in Abbey Street.

"Thank God you're an American sailor Jerome, Jaysus at first I thought you were one of dem Balubas."

The young sailor looked at Eddie, puzzled. "A what buddy?" he asked. "What the hell are you talking about? What the heck's a Baluba?"

"Ah nuthin," replied Eddie. "Me brother Paddy; he was in the army, the Irish army over in Africa and was killed by the Balubas, fecker's ate him up so they did. Forget about it, it doesn't matter anymore."

As they reached the steps leading down to the basement club big Frankie Coyle the bouncer blocked Eddie's way.

"How yeh Frankie?" said Eddie. "Who's playing tonight?"

"Ah some crowd called Grannies Intentions," replied big Frankie. "Crowd of fuckin bog trotters up from Limerick. I hear they're shite. Anyway, Kelly, where the fuck do yeh think you're going pal with that black sailor? You're not getting in here with him so you're not. Do yeh hear me now pal? So scarper. Fuck off, dem black sailors," he continued, "they always cause rows so fuck off now Kelly."

Eddie protested. "Ah for Jaysus sake Frankie let's in. Don't fuck up me Friday night. I'll look after the sailor fella so I will, all me mates are down there, so is me bird, so give us a feckin break for Jaysus sake Frankie let's bleedin in will yeh. I promise there'll be no trouble. I'll look after him so I will."

"I said fuck off Kelly and I bleedin meant it," replied Frankie. "You're not getting in here with your man there and dat's dat pal. So fuck off before I bleedin burst yeh."

Jerome turned to Eddie. "It's okay buddy. You go on. I don't want to mess up your night."

"It's alright Jerome," Eddie replied. "Let's go. I wouldn't give that fat bastard the satisfaction."

As they turned and crossed the street big Frankie shouted. "Hey, Kelly, yeh better watch yourself with dat black fella, he might chop you up and eat yeh like dem blackies ate your brother Paddy."

Eddie turned and shouted, "Ah fuck off, yeh fat cunt."

As they walked away Jerome turned to Eddie and asked, "Hey buddy where can a thirsty guy get a drink in this town?"

"Not a chance in hell. The pubs are closed and none of the club's sell drink. Anyway you probably won't get in, what with you being a sailor and all dat, no offence, pal. Fuck this," Eddie continued. "Dat's me Friday night ruined so I might as well start walking home to Finglas."

Jerome put his arm around Eddie and said, "Hey buddy I tell you what; the night's young. How would you like to come back to my ship for a beer or two? I think I can swing it to get you on board. My buddy Sonny is on night watch tonight, he's from my home town Detroit. What do you say buddy, we're not allowed booze on the ship but all the officer's are on shore-leave tonight, at some fancy ball or something, they won't be back until the early hours. The sailor's who didn't get shore-leave have organised a secret party with booze we smuggled from the States."

"Jaysus! Brilliant!" said Eddie. "I've never been on a warship before, more booze and a bit of feckin excitement, absolutely brilliant! Massive!"

They walked back down O'Connell's Street and turned down the quays towards the North Wall and the docks chatting and joking. Suddenly out of the darkness a huge ship appeared with blazing lights, the reflection of the ships' lights bouncing on the dark flowing waters of the Liffey. The illuminations of the ship reminded Eddie of the bright lights of a carnival lit up at night and he felt a great sense of excitement as he approached the ship.

A black sailor, wearing a white uniform and carrying a baton stepped forward. Jerome greeted the sailor. "My main man Sonny. What's cooking, brother?"

Eddie looked on, amazed at the black sailor's funny way of talking.

"It's okay Eddie, everything's cool buddy, welcome to my home, welcome on board the USS Neptune and by the way this is my best buddy Sonny." Eddie shook the young sailor's hand warmly.

As Eddie walked up the gangplank he couldn't believe his eyes. Everything looked and sounded absolutely wonderful, from the shiny metal and the big guns, to the ships' lights bouncing off the water and the humming sound from the generator in the background. Jerome led Eddie down a narrow metal staircase and along a dimly lit corridor to a noisy room full of sailors, mainly black faces with just one or two white ones, barely visible in the smoke-filled room. Eddie followed Jerome through the crowd and over to a small makeshift bar. Jerome shouted, "Hey guys, this is Eddie, he's my buddy. He's a local so look after him and by the way he's an undertaker's assistant so watch it; Eddie's always on the lookout for new business." They all laughed.

The sailors crowded around Eddie. Eddie's was the first strange face they'd seen in weeks. "Hey, buddy," asked the sailor behind the bar. "What will yeh have to drink?"

Eddie replied, "Dat's very kind of yis. I'll have me usual, thank you kindly pal—a pint of Guinness if yeh don't mind."

The sailor's laughed. "Guinness, buddy? What the heck is Guinness?"

"Sorry buddy," said the barman. "No funny drinks on this ship."

Jerome said, "Hey, guys, you'll never believe what these guys drink here in Ireland. This Guinness stuff, it's black. A black beer."

None of the sailors had ever heard of a drink called Guinness and they couldn't believe that the drink was black.

The sailor manning the makeshift bar shook hands with Eddie. "Buddy you can have a choice of Colt 45, Budweiser, Milwaukee or the hard stuff, Jack Daniels or Southern Comfort, just name your poison."

Eddie was dumbfounded. In the Ace of Spades it was a pint of Guinness or Smithwick's Ale, or if you were lucky at Christmas, a Powers whiskey with peppermint. "Right," he replied. "I'll start with the very first one, whatever yeh call it ,and work me way through to the very last one, dat way I'll miss nuthin and find out which one I like the best."

The sailor's all laughed.

He started with a Colt 45. "Lovely stuff," said Eddie as he stood beside the bar surrounded by a sea of friendly faces. He felt like a king, for the first time in his life he was the centre of attention and as he got drunker he got more relaxed and he liked the Lucky Strike American cigarettes – nice flavour, very tasty.

He started to tell the sailors all the undertaker's jokes that he hated so much. They loved his funny accent and the way he talked. Eddie loved the attention, he was on a roll; so he began to tell them all about Dublin and the pubs and the characters and all about Shaky Shanahan. He never mentioned the Balubas in case some of them were related.

One of the white sailor's introduced himself. "Hi Eddie," he said. "I'm Ned O'Brien one of the ship's cooks. My folk's came from the Emerald Isle. What about a rebel song buddy? My grandma used to sing rebel songs when we were kids back home in Somerville Boston you gotta know a rebel song Eddie."

Eddie felt like king of the castle. He took a long swig from his Jack Daniels (he was on the American whiskey now) and thought hard about what song he could sing. He never sang rebel songs, he hated all that Irish rebel bullshit but he did remember the one song he'd been taught by his ma when he was a child. It was about James Connolly. He and Paddy used to sing it for Florrie and Greta when they visited the house in Sandymount. Eddie couldn't sing a note but he closed his eyes, his voice well lubricated by the large amount of Yankee gargle he had consumed, and broke into song in a slightly nervous voice:

A great crowd had gathered outside of Kilmainham.
With their heads all uncovered, they knelt on the ground.

For inside that grim prison lay a brave Irish soldier.
His life for his country about to lay down.

He went to his death like a true son of Ireland.
The firing party he bravely did face.

Then the order rang out "Present arms, Fire."
James Connolly fell into a ready-made grave.

The black flag they hoisted, the cruel deed was over.
Gone was the man that loved Ireland so well.

There was many a sad heart in Dublin that morning,
When they murdered James Connolly the Irish rebel.

Many years have gone by since the Irish rebellion,
When the guns of Britannia they loudly did speak.

And the bold Irish Army they stood shoulder to shoulder,
And the blood from their bodies flowed down Sackville Street

The General Post Office, the English bombarded, the spirit
Of freedom they tried hard to quell,

But above all the din came, came the cry, "No surrender."
Twa's the voice of James Connolly, the Irish rebel.

Eddie felt emotional as he sang and tears began to roll down his cheeks when he finished. He had never sung the song before in public and it brought all the sad memories of his childhood flooding back. There was a moments silence in the room then

53

sudden applause from the sailors. They hadn't a clue what the young Dublin lad was singing about but those Irish rebel songs sure sounded pretty good to them.

The hours passed quickly and Eddie got drunker and drunker, it was the best night of his life. He couldn't wait till he got home to tell his ma all about the American warship and the sailors he had met.

When the ship's bell rang one o'clock Eddie tried to stand up. "Jaysus lads," he said. "Jaysus lads I better be getting home now me ould one will be waiting up for me so she will." As he got off the stool the room began to spin around and everything started to get blurred then he blacked out.

"Eddie are you okay buddy?" asked Jerome, as he tried to grab Eddie before he collapsed in a heap on the deck. "Guys" said Jerome. "We've got to get Eddie off the ship. The officer's will be back soon. If any of the officer's find him onboard we're in deep shit." They tried to lift Eddie's crumpled heap off the deck and get him to the gangplank but it was impossible. Eddie had passed out in a deep drunken stupor unable to move. All evidence of the bar and the alcohol were quickly removed.

"Tell you what guys," Jerome shouted to his companions. "Hide Eddie in the dry store off the galley, we can smuggle him off the ship at daybreak, there's a party going ashore for fresh provisions. We can smuggle him off first thing in the morning without anyone noticing." Several of the sailor's dragged the drunken Eddie into a small store off the galley where he lay in a drunken stupor snoring on the cold metal deck of the ship.

OSTRICHES

Bridie let Eddie have a lie-in every Saturday morning and this Saturday morning was no exception. At about twelve o'clock she went to his bedroom to wake him up. He wasn't there. She was shocked. This was the first time that Eddie had not come home after a Friday night out; no matter how drunk he was he always came home. Something was wrong; she instinctively knew it. She had the same awful feeling the night Paddy was killed. She remembered it well, the night she had that terrible dream and Sweet Jaysus she would never forget that dream to the day she died. It was in Africa where Paddy was serving in the army. She was standing in a field of fruit trees, all coloured fruit, yellow, red and a lovely sweet smell, like the smell in a fruit shop. It was a beautiful calm sunny day when suddenly hundreds of bird's came running into the field, big bird's with long legs, long necks – funny looking birds. She laughed. Yes, she had seen bird's like that before. Yes, ostriches, that's what they were called – ostriches. She saw them once before up in Dublin Zoo. She had taken Paddy and Eddie up to the zoo during the school holidays and the two boys were in hysterics rolling around laughing at the funny looking birds with their long legs and long necks.

Something was wrong, she stopped smiling. The bird's were running amok, frantically running into each other and wildly crashing into the trees. When she looked closely, she knew something was wrong; something terrible was wrong. Sweet Jaysus, the bird's had no heads. Their necks were sewn over. They banged their headless necks and bodies madly at the trees, kicking their feet, going crazy and running into each other in a blind panic. It was horrible. She woke up suddenly gasping for breath, her body covered in sweat and she started to cry. She knew her first-born son was dead; her Paddy was gone and she knew he had died in agony, crying out for her. She could hear the desperate screams of her son. "Mammy! Mammy! Jaysus

Mary and Joseph, help me, Mammy! Help me!" And him lying there in some faraway place under the blazing sun, amongst strangers with no one to help him. Her poor son. Her beloved first-born son Paddy.

She went to the box room and tried frantically to wake Seamy from his drunken slumber, to tell him something terrible had happened to Paddy but she couldn't wake him. He just lay there snoring and mumbling in his sleep. Tears streamed down her face as she went down the stairs in the darkness. She lit a cigarette and as she put the kettle on the gas cooker to make a cup of tea, the silence of the night was broken by a loud knock on the front door. The knock had come sooner than she had expected. The young army despatch rider stood nervously on the doorstep in a long, green, military overcoat.

"Missus Kelly?" he said quietly without looking Bridie in the eye. "I've got some bad news; it's your son, Private Patrick Christopher Kelly." He handed her an official looking brown envelope with a harp symbol.

"He's dead isn't he?" asked Bridie. "He's been killed, hasn't he?"

The young soldier looked down uneasily at his dull reflection on his shiny, brown, polished army boots. "Yes, Missus Kelly," he replied without looking up. "He died for his country. Killed in action over in Katanga in the Congo."

Bridie fainted. When she woke up she was a different person; a part of her had died that night somewhere far away in a lonely distant place under the blazing African sun; part of her had died with her first-born son.

When Seamy heard the news about Paddy he headed straight down to his local pub the Drake Inn to drown his sorrows, he was still drowning his sorrows at closing time that night, paralytic drunk from all the free pints of Guinness. Seamy got a lot of mileage from the death of his first-born son, the hero of the Congo.

Where the hell is Eddie? Bridie thought as she rushed down the stairs to the living room. Seamy was sitting at the table as usual reading the racing page of the Evening Herald. "What's up? What's the story?" he asked, without glancing up from his paper.

"It's Eddie he never came home last night. Something terrible has happened to him. He's never stayed out before. I'm worried sick, something's happened to him, I just know it has, Seamy for Christ's sake what am I going to do I'm at me wit's end so I am?"

"I couldn't give a fuck about what you're going to do missus" Seamy replied, anger in his voice. "But I'll can tell yeh what I'm going to do so I will I'm going to fuckin kill the ungrateful little bollix when I get my hands on him after all I've done for him, I'll swing for the little fucker so I will . The dirty bleedin ungrateful bastard fucked off to England, I always knew he would" Seamy continued without looking up from his paper, "Over to dat pal of his, what do you call him now? Gary Monks dat's it, the big lanky fucker, he ran off to London didn't he, no fuckin monk dat fella, I can tell yeh dat for nuthin, deserting his poor ma and da like dat, and I can tell yeh something for else for nuthin, dat's exactly what your son has done missus – fucked off to England leaving us here to starve to death. I always knew he was a good for nuthin lazy bastard. I'll fuckin throttle the fucker when I get me hands on him so I will and after all the things I've done for him, I just can't believe it."

Bridie hadn't listened to a word he'd said and headed out the door. She knew Eddie would never leave her. No not Eddie; he was too good, too thoughtful and kind; her special little funny cuts would never abandon his poor mother. No something terrible was wrong. She knew it. She just knew it.

She walked the short distance to Anto O'Toole's house in Casement Drive, just around the corner. Anto was Eddie's best friend. As she walked up the garden path the front door opened and a smiling face greeted her. It was Anto's mother.

"How are yeh Bridie? What's up?"

"It's Eddie Mary. He never came home last night. I'm worried sick about him so I am. I was wondering if your Anthony knows where he is. He was with him last night."

Mary turned and shouted up the stairs. "Anthony will yeh ever get up out of that bleedin bed for the love of Sweet Jaysus. It's Eddie's mammy. She's looking for him; he never came home last night. Do yeh know where he is?"

Minutes later, a bleary eyed Anto – dishevelled hair, smelling of drink and dressed only in his soiled under-pants – struggled down the stairs.

"Howya, Missus Kelly?" he said sleepily. "What's the story? What's up?"

"It's Eddie, Anthony. He never came home last night. Do you know where he is? I'm worried sick so I am. Have yeh any idea where he might be Anthony?"

"Jaysus, I'm sorry, Missus Kelly. I haven't got a clue where he is. He never came to the Go-Go club last night. He never showed up and we were all wondering where he was. Even Colette Murphy was going crazy looking for him. But he didn't miss much only some culchie band from Limerick although I thought they were very good, loved the soul and Motown music and the singer was brilliant so he was, but some of the crowd from Finglas didn't like them, they prefer the blues' music so a big fight broke out so it did. Big Frankie the bouncer went crazy with a bleedin hammer. He nearly killed a couple of lads. Jaysus, there was blood everywhere. It was brilliant; although your Eddie wouldn't have liked it. He hates' fights so he does."

What Eddie Kelly would never know was that Colette Murphy had waited anxiously all that Friday night and early Saturday morning for him to arrive at the Go-Go club. She had something very special in mind for Eddie that night, something very special indeed.

The previous Monday morning, Colette Murphy's best friend Imelda Ryan had arrived at work in Woolworths in Henry Street all excited.

"Colette," she said. "You're never going to believe it; I did it with Mickser on Saturday night. It was feckin mighty so it was, Jaysus Colette. It was feckin great."

"Did what?" asked Colette, a surprised look on her face.

"I did it Colette. I let Mickser go all the way; I let him ride me so I did."

"Ah no Imelda, yeh didn't? How could yeh, yeh dirty bitch? I can't believe what you're saying."

"It was great Colette. It was bleedin massive."

"Where did yis do it?"

"In the park beside the canal on the way home from the Go-Go club. He dragged me behind the bushes and pulled me knickers off. It was so romantic. Jaysus the size of his bleedin mickey Colette; it was bleeding huge. Jaysus, I get the bleedin shivers just thinking about it. He was like a feckin wild animal so he was; like a bleedin dog in heat."

Colette was shocked. "Did it hurt?" she asked curiously. "No not a bit. It was brilliant. We're in love. He's going to marry me. Isn't it great Colette?"

"What if yeh get pregnant?"

"So bleedin what? We'll run off to England and get married, we love each other and dat's all that matters. Listen Colette. I'll tell yeh something for nuthin'; if yeh love Eddie and yeh want to keep him yeh better let him ride yeh because if yeh won't let him ride yeh he'll get some other bird down in the Go-Go club who will some Friday night. Just yeh wait and see Colette Murphy."

Colette was shocked.

"If she gets pregnant he'll have to marry her and where does that leave you? Do yeh see what I mean Colette? Yeh better get thinking about it."

All that week Colette couldn't stop thinking about it. She knew she loved Eddie Kelly; she always loved him. She knew they would get married some day. She knew he loved her, yes she would; she'd let him ride her on Friday night after the Go-Go club, yes she'd let her Eddie go all the way. If she got pregnant sure she knew he'd marry her, they were made for each other. Her heart raced. She couldn't wait till Saturday night. *Jaysus,* she thought, *I'll have to get a new pair of knickers in Clearys, something fancy, something to get his heart racing and his micky standing up, all hard and tall like Nelson's pillar.* She couldn't sleep a wink all that week. She was so excited. She couldn't wait until Friday night.

Bridie's heart sank. "So you didn't see him, Anthony? You don't know where he is?"

"Sorry Missus Kelly about Eddie, but I haven't got a clue where he is. But I'll tell you what; I'll ask around and if I hear anything I will give you a shout, alright?"

"Thanks Anthony. I appreciate your help." She turned and walked down the path and made her way down towards the village and Finglas Garda station.

Sergeant Molloy was on duty behind the reception desk as Bridie entered the dingy police station. The big sergeant looked up from the newspaper he was reading. "Good day to you missus," he said warmly. "What can I do you for?" But when he read Bridie's face he knew he had been insensitive. He could see she was troubled. "Can I help you, mam?" he asked sympathy in his voice. "Tell me now what's troubling you."

"It's me son Garda," said Bridie. "He's gone missing; he never came home last night." "Come over here now missus," said Sergeant Molloy in a kind voice. "Sit down here and tell me the story, start at the beginning and tell me everything now nice and slow."

Between outbursts of sobbing Bridie told the sergeant the whole story about her father and how he died fighting the English and about Paddy's death in Africa and finally all about Eddie and his disappearance. When she finished, an hour later, Sergeant Molloy stood up.

"For God's sake Missus Kelly. The young fella has only gone for one night; you know what these young fellas are like nowadays. He probably got off with some bird or something and that's where the young scallywag is. I'm sure of it so I am. That's what the little fecker is doing missus, sowing his wild oats, trying to get his leg over somewhere if you know what I mean. There's nothing to worry about he'll show up soon enough so he will just you wait and see, for God's sake he's only missing for one night."

"Listen I'll tell you what I'll do Missus Kelly. I'll make a few phone calls to see if anything turns up. I'll call up to your house – 38 Kildonan Parade you said it was? – If I hear anything at all, now don't you worry about a thing? Everything will be all right so it will just you wait and see." "Thank you Garda," replied Bridie and left to walk the short distance across the fields to her house. The sergeant's kind words however had given her not one bit of comfort at all.

By the end of the week she was at her wit's end. She spent hours praying every day to Saint Anthony in Saint Canice's church in the village and what little money she had lighting candles and begging the saint to bring Eddie home safely but her prayers went unanswered.

Every day after church she called into the Garda station to see if they had any news but is was always the same. By Friday Sergeant Molloy began to share Bridie's concern.

He rang the city morgue and all the hospitals to try to get something on Eddie Kelly but without any success. He finally reported Eddie as a missing person to Garda headquarters. *It was very strange*, he thought, *all very strange, very strange indeed.* Finally he came to the conclusion that Eddie had ran off to England and deserted his mother; gone in search of the bright lights, looking for wine, women and song, and *who could blame the young lad?* The sergeant privately thought. *He didn't have much of a life here in Dublin now, did he? And sure when the novelty wore off he'd come home. Sure, didn't they all?*

That Friday afternoon, a week to the day that her son Eddie Kelly had gone missing, Bridie took a bus down to Finlater's Place to see Shaky Shanahan to find out if he knew anything about Eddie's disappearance.

When Bridie walked into the undertakers Shaky started to give off about Eddie. "Listen, missus," he said angrily. "Dat feckin son of yours has let me down badly. I can't run this place by myself if yeh know what I mean. I know you're hard up missus but I'll have to sack him if he doesn't turn up soon, where the feck is he anyway?"

Bridie started to cry. "He's gone missing Shaky. He went out last Friday night and he hasn't been seen since. I'm worried sick about him Shaky, what am I going to do? I've spoken to the Garda but they know nothing so they don't they can't find him Shaky. I'm worried sick about me son can you help me? For the love of sweet Jaysus Shaky can yeh help me? I have to find him. It was bad enough losing Paddy but Eddie too? Oh Jaysus I can't bear to think about it so I can't he's all I have to live for and I miss him so much Shaky he's all I have in the world so he is."

Shaky felt sorry for Bridie. "What do you mean he never came home? He couldn't have just disappeared off the face of the earth now missus could he?"

Bridie told Shaky what his father and even the Garda suspected. "His father and his pals and even Sergeant Molloy in Finglas Garda station think he's run off to England and dat's the story, so it is. For the love of God will you help me Shaky? You're me last hope. I have nowhere else to turn I know you like Eddie Shaky you're like a father to him so yeh are, he thinks the world of yeh so he does."

He listened carefully to Bridie's words. *She's right,* he thought. *No, there's no way, no way at all, Eddie would run off to England and leave his mother or his job. No there was no way he would do that without saying something first.* Shaky knew the full measure of Eddie Kelly, he was a good lad, a gentle lad, devoted to his mother; he saw much kindness in him, a lad who wouldn't hurt a fly. *Yes,* he thought, *something has happened to Eddie. He can't have just disappeared off the face of the earth.*

"Bridie are you sure the Garda can do nothing? Surely they can find out something. Jaysus Bridie you can't just vanish off the face of the earth now can yeh. Listen here," he continued. "Take this." He slipped a few pounds into Bridie's hand. It was his drinking money for the weekend but he knew she was in more need of it. "Go home now missus and I'll see what I can do. I'll tell you what; I'll go and make a few enquires for you so

I will. I'll speak to a few people I know who might be able to help. I'll get to the bottom of this Bridie I promise yeh dat so I do."

As he watched her small sad huddled figure crossing the street to catch the number forty bus home to Finglas he thought, *Jaysus the Lord Almighty is awful hard on some poor creatures so he is. Whatever his reason, poor Bridie Kelly has more than her fair share of crosses to bear. First her father killed in the 16 rising and then poor Paddy and now this. Sometimes I wonder what the man above is thinking so I do.* Shaky went back into the funeral home, lit a Woodbine, and sat down on a coffin. *Well,* he thought, *dat's me drinking for the weekend put to bed but sure I can cadge a few gargles here and there but sure what the heck.* He was glad he had helped poor Bridie. He pulled hard on his cigarette and wondered what he could do to find out what happened to Eddie. He was sure he hadn't run off to England. No definitely not; he would never leave his mother not without saying something first. Something must have happened to him. He had to find him. He had to put Bridie out of her misery. Shaky knew that if there was one man alive in the whole of Dublin City who could find Eddie Kelly it was Basher Brannigan. Detective Basher Brannigan, Dublin Special Branch.

Marble Slabs

Later that evening Shaky Shanahan left Finlater's Place walked down Henry Street and headed towards the headquarters of the Garda Special Branch in the Bridewell just off the quays. As he turned into Jervis Street he stopped and looked at the tall imposing red brick building that was Jervis Street Hospital. That's where it had all began for Shaky Shanahan as an undertaker. He'd started out with his father as an undertaker's assistant at the age of twelve working out of their old premises in the Liberties before they moved to Finlater's Place. He remembered Jervis Street Hospital very well, how could he ever forget those terrible nights all those year's ago? It was Easter 1916, the Republicans and the Citizen's Army were fighting the English all over the city and Dublin was burning. The parish priest in the Liberties had asked his father to go and collect the bodies of the dead and injured lying in the streets and bring them to Jervis Street Hospital. Their horse, frightened by the noise of gunfire, couldn't be tethered so Shaky and his father pulled an open cart through the streets in the darkness collecting the dead and the wounded and taking them to Jervis Street. He and his father helping the nurses and doctors lift the dead and the wounded from the cart and carry the dead down to the mortuary in the basement of the hospital.

He vividly remembered the bodies lying on the marble slabs all burnt and shot; their bloody wounds and blackened faces illuminated in the flickering gas light. How could he ever forget those terrible nights and the crying of the injured women and children? On several occasions they were nearly killed when the Republicans opened fire on them, mistaking them for the English soldiers in the dark.

Once, up in King Street near Smithfield, they picked up a dying young English soldier and lay him on the cart next to the body of a Citizen's Army Volunteer – only boys. Behind the uniform it didn't matter; they still left behind their poor families to pick up the pieces. The futile waste of life, the terrible suffering. He would never, ever, as long as he lived forget the awful things he saw that night. Maybe that's why he drank so much, to erase the horrible memories of it all. Like his father he abhorred violence for whatever cause. It was always the poor that suffered – men killing men and for what? An Irish Republic, for freedom? Christ it all made him sick. The poor were still poor and the rich were still rich. All that tragic death and destruction? Bloody idiots the lot of them. He wondered what the high and mighty Pearse in his fancy uniform would think about the poor old people dying today of cold and hunger. Christ the number of destitute old people he'd had to bury over the years it was appalling. And all the young men and women having to emigrate to England and beyond to find work. Then they divide the country. Some bloody Republic it turned out to be. He recalled his father saying that the English bosses were bad but the Irish ones were even worse. What's the difference, an Irish flag or an English one? All the same. *Yeh can't feed a flag to a hungry child. A curse on the lot of the murdering bastards.* No he had no time for priests. He hadn't been to church since his father died. *Them and their bloody religion.* Although he did have to admit that he had some respect, but only a little, for James Connolly. He did try to help the working classes but then he had to join the Republicans and take up arms. *The stupid rebellion destroying Dublin, all the shooting and the killing.* This only added to the suffering of the poor, made things even worse.

He entered the dark forbidden interior of the Bridewell, nodded to the duty sergeant, and climbed slowly up the rickety, narrow, timber staircase to the detective's room at the end of the dimly lit corridor. As he entered the large room Detective Basher Brannigan glanced up from behind his desk partly concealed by a pile of cluttered papers and dusty files. He smiled at Shaky. "Jaysus Mary and Joseph would yeh ever look at what the cat dragged in. Holy God Almighty, if it isn't old Shaky Shanahan, friend of the living and friend of the dead. Sit down, Shaky. Sit down," he said warmly and pointed to the chair in the corner. "Pull over a chair. Sit down and rest your weary limbs. Great to see yeh so it is always nice to see old Shaky Shanahan." Brannigan produced two tea stained mugs and a bottle of Powers whiskey. "Here wet your whistle on a drop of the hard stuff Shaky and tell me what's up, Jaysus yeh look like you've just come from a funeral so yeh do."

Shaky didn't smile. The big detective knew something was up; the little undertaker was normally game for a laugh. Shaky took a long swig of the whiskey and said, "Seriously, Basher, I've got a problem and I need your help. It's really important; will yeh help me, Mister Brannigan?"

The detective looked hard at the diminutive figure that sat before him. He liked Shaky Shanahan. He dressed in his shabby clothes with that awful smell. He remembered many years ago when he was promoted off the beat and transferred into the Special Branch to work on what they called the dead shift. When a body was found at night in Dublin city, it was his job to go to the scene and arrange the removal of the corpse and sometimes organise the funeral. Most of the cases he handled were old people, usually in winter, when they had died of hunger and the cold. The bodies often lay unnoticed for weeks before they were found – poor old creatures, paupers without money for food or heat and because they had no money they were usually without family or friends so the state had to arrange and pay for the funeral. But the money the state paid was never enough for most of the big Dublin undertakers and it would take months for the meagre payment to come through. So that was how he had met Shaky Shanahan – the only undertaker in Dublin willing to bury the poor old folk on state credit and for a paltry sum. Once or twice Shaky had buried unidentified persons, usually tramps or alcoholics, without payment. Brannigan had asked him to do it. Shaky had always obliged him – decent old sod. Now he had a chance to help Shaky – payback time for all his kindness, for all he had done for the poor old paupers. Yes he would gladly help the little man. *Favour's given, favour's returned.*

"Okay Shaky," he said. "Give me the whole story now, start at the very beginning and finish at the very end, now off yeh go."

The undertaker spoke non-stop for almost an hour telling him the whole story pausing only to take intermittent swigs of whiskey. Detective Brannigan listened to every word intently without speaking his detective's mind already shifting and sorting out the facts. When Shaky finally finished the detective stood up shook his hand and said, "Okay, I've got the story. I'll leave no stone unturned. I promise you Shaky I'll find Eddie Kelly. Mark my words I'll find him, dead or alive."

The dead bit unnerved Shaky "Thanks Basher," he said. "I know you'll find Eddie, I know you will, I have every confidence in you detective so I have. Please do what yeh can for his unfortunate mother's sake? I'll tell you what Basher," he continued, "I owe you one. You won't have to dip your hand into your pocket at your own funeral; it won't cost you a penny. It's on the house detective."

As Shaky turned and left Brannigan smiled, he was glad to see Shaky had got some of his good humour back; that was a good sign, a good omen.

Now, he thought, *let's get to work. Let's find Eddie Kelly before his mother dies of a broken heart. Let's get to the bottom of this little mystery.*

He left the Bridewell and walked quickly down the quays along Bachelor's Walk, towards the Ace of Spades public house, a week to the night that young Kelly had disappeared.

BANK ROBBERS

As he walked down the quays, the odd passer-by would see him and glance away quickly avoiding eye contact. He had a reputation as a hard chaw, a tough man who took no nonsense, feared by the criminal classes of Dublin. His fearsome reputation had begun at the time of the bank robbery many years before. He was a young Garda just up from the country, from Annally in County Longford, a rookie cop out on the beat before he got promoted to the Special Branch. One day a woman ran up to him and shouted, "Garda! Garda! Quick! There's a robbery going on across the road in the Munster and Leinster Bank." Garda Brannigan calmly walked across the road and entered the bank. People were lying on the floor and two masked men with shotguns were raiding the tills. The gunmen turned and pointed their guns at him. He walked up to the gunmen without any sign of fear and calmly said, "Okay lads the game's up. Now give me dem feckin guns before someone gets hurt." The robbers couldn't believe what they were hearing. But there was something about the big cop that made them freeze, something in his cold eyes.

To the astonishment of the frightened customers the two robbers put their shotguns on the counter and timidly gave themselves up. He became headline news his photograph on the front page of the Evening Herald. Garda Brannigan became the hero of Dublin.

He was taken off the beat and out of uniform, promoted to detective Special Branch and moved to the dead shift at the Special Branch Headquarters in the Bridewell.

He reached the Ace of Spades and walked into the crowded bar. A hush came over the noisy pub. Basher walked straight up to the bar counter and called the barman. "Hey chief, were you working here last Friday night?"

"Yes," replied Terry. "I never leave this spot detective. Chained to the bar, that's what I am, chained to the bar. What's up? Can I help yeh? By the way would yeh like a quick one? It's on the house detective."

Brannigan ignored the offer. "Chief," asked Basher, "Do you know a young fella, name of Kelly, Eddie Kelly from out Finglas direction? He drinks here."

"Yeh I know him very well," the barman replied. "Come's in here every Friday night without fail." He glanced around. "Although funny enough, he's not here tonight. He never usually misses a Friday night. He sits on that very bar stool there beside you detective and sit's there all night smiling at himself in the mirror. That's why all the old fellas here call him Smiler Kelly. Anyway detective as I was saying he sits right there on that very stool and gets drunk. Harmless lad all the same; an undertaker's assistant, that's what he is, works for that feckin head the ball, what do yeh call him now? That ould eejit yeh Shaky Shanahan, that's it. Why Detective? Has something happened to him?"

"Was he here last Friday night, chief?" asked Basher.

"Yes so he was," replied Terry. "Nothing unusual, same as always."

"Did anything strange happen that night?" asked Basher. "Anything at all out of the ordinary?"

"No I don't think so detective," replied Terry. "Same as always – drink, drink and more drink, sorry I can't help you, Mister Brannigan."

Basher turned without replying and headed towards the door. As he pushed open the heavy pub doors the barman suddenly shouted, "Hey detective, come over here a minute, I do remember something that might help. Last Friday night a black fella came in here, as black as your boot so he was. He got talking to young Kelly and they left the bar together, both of them were a bit drunk. The black fella, he was wearing a uniform, I think he might have been a sailor from the docks."

"Do yeh know where they went chief?" asked Brannigan.

"I haven't got a got a clue detective, but the Kelly fella, he always went around to that dump – what do yeh call it? Yeh hippie heaven, happy home of the long haired freaks – the Go-Go Beat Club, opposite Wynn's Hotel in Abbey Street, after he leaves here."

"Thanks chief," said Basher as he left the Ace of Spades. He quickly walked up the quays towards O' Connell's Bridge turning right at O'Connell's Street and onto Abbey Street. The streets were crowded with people, young couples arm in arm, smiling and laughing, out on the town, heading to the bars and clubs just like Eddie Kelly the previous week. As he crossed Abbey Street and walked towards the Go-Go beat club, big Frankie the bouncer marched up and down on sentry duty at the top of the narrow stone steps that led down to the basement club. He felt his stomach churn.

Christ! He thought. *It's that big, ugly mug, culchie cop, Basher Brannigan. Jaysus, I'm fucked. I'll go down for years for this one.*

Basher grabbed Frankie by the arm. "Okay, chief, I need some information. It's very important now."

Big Frankie instantly panicked. "Jaysus Mr Brannigan, it was all an accident, a terrible mistake. It wasn't deliberate; it was all dem feckin hippies fault."

Basher looked surprised. What the hell was big Frankie talking about? "What hippies, in God's name, what the fuck are yeh on about?" asked Brannigan?

"Dem hippies last week. They attacked me, three of them, Mr Brannigan. I had to defend meself. Dat's all it was, pure self defence. I had to do something Mr. Brannigan. It was the first fella, a big, ugly long-haired fucker from Finglas, he attacked me so I hit him with me hammer so I did, yeh know, the one I always carry for self defence. Yeh know what I mean, Mister Brannigan; this is a very dangerous job so it is, now to tell yeh the truth," he continued, "I did glass the other bastard with a broken bottle in the face but again it was purely in self defence, I swear it on me mother's life so I do. And furthermore I swear on me granny's life that I didn't mean to give him forty stitches. It was self-defence dat's all it was Mister Brannigan pure self-defence; I had to protect meself so I had. Anyway it was all dat fuckin band from Limerick's fault and their singer, a big, ugly, serious-looking culchie with a head like a fuckin turnip: Johnny Dunne I think they call him. Anyway the crowd didn't like dem and those hippy fellas I was telling you about, Mister Brannigan, they wanted their money back. No fuckin way were they getting their money back? No fuckin way, the boss wouldn't have any of dat so he wouldn't. Anyway dat's how the row started. It was all the fault of dat feckin Limerick band. Grannies Intentions? Did yeh ever hear such a bleedin stupid name in all your fuckin life Mister Brannigan? Grannies Intentions?" Frankie laughed. "Grannies fuckin Intentions, where the fuck did they get a stupid name like dat, in a bleedin lucky bag?" As he looked at the detective, Frankie suddenly stopped speaking. There was a look in the detective's eye. "Mister Brannigan," he asked, "Yeh are here about the big fight last Friday night aren't yeh? Yeh are here to arrest me, aren't yeh, Mister Brannigan?"

Basher ignored Frankie's question and said, "Listen chief do you know a young fella called Eddie Kelly from Finglas, was he here last week, have you seen him at all?"

"I know him alright but he's not here tonight, well not yet anyway, detective. In fact the last time I saw him was last – eh, let me think – yeh, last Friday night. Eh, yeh, just before the big fight.Yeh your right, he was here last week, he was with a black fella that looked like a sailor off the ships so he did. Jaysus, wasn't it, eh, funny, Mister Brannigan, the way Kelly's brother was eaten by dem black fellas out in Africa, the Balubas?" A smile lit up on his face. "As I was saying, Mister Brannigan; last Friday night Eddie Kelly was here with a black sailor, but I wouldn't let him in to the club. No, no bleedin way, not with a black fella; they always start fights dem fellas; they're very violent yeh know Mister Brannigan dem black fellas. Sure look what happened to Kelly's bleedin brother."

"Do you know where he went when he left here?"

"He walked across Abbey Street towards O'Connell's Bridge, the black fella was with him but I haven't seen him since. Why?" asked Frankie, a smile on his face. "Is something up? What's the story Mister Brannigan? Did the black fella gobble him up or what?"

Brannigan turned and walked away without replying and just before he reached the corner of O'Connell's Street he turned around to Frankie and shouted, "I hope I have the full story do you hear me now chief? If I find out you're lying I'll be back here with a warrant for your arrest, have yeh got the message now chief?"

"Absolutely, Mister Brannigan. Absolutely. Would I lie to you Mister Brannigan? "

As soon as Basher was out of sight big Frankie looked around carefully to make sure nobody was near. When he was absolutely sure that there was no one was within earshot he muttered to himself, "Big bollix! Big fuckin culché, bog-trottin bollix."

Detective Brannigan nodded to the duty sergeant and headed up the stairs to his dark empty office. Without turning on the lights he opened the drawer of his desk and pulled out a half-full bottle of Powers Irish whiskey. He poured a large measure into his tea stained mug and stood looking down at the dark waters of the river Liffey below, silently flowing towards the docks and Dublin Bay. He liked the night shift. He liked the silence and he liked the darkness. He didn't much like people. He was a loner. In some ways preferring the company of dead people. They never caused any trouble; it was the living that caused all the pain and the hurt.

He sipped at his whiskey and began to consider all the fact's about Eddie Kelly's disappearance. First of all he couldn't give a shit about the hippies big Frankie was on about; they deserved everything they got. Jaysus he hated those hippie fuckers – scruffy looking cunts with their long hair; look more like fuckin women than men; no respect for themselves at all; drop outs; worse than animals those dirty fuckers; fair play to big Frankie. Anyway back to Eddie Kelly. He agreed with Shaky Shanahan; the young fella didn't run off to England, not without saying something first. No, no way. Not hard enough. Much too soft. No, definitely not England he wouldn't leave his mother. He wouldn't have the fucking balls. He had established that young Kelly had gone out last Friday night as usual and spent most of the night in his local pub the Ace of Spades. He then went around as usual to the Go-Go club in Abbey Street but couldn't get in because of the black sailor. *That was it. Yes*, he thought. That was the only thing unusual about Eddie Kelly's Friday night routine, the presence of the black sailor. Big Frankie and the barman both said that the black fella was wearing a uniform, a sailor. So Eddie Kelly meets a black sailor and couldn't get into that kip, the Go-Go club, and was last seen heading towards O'Connell's Bridge with the black sailor. Then he disappears, not a trace, not a word. The duty sergeant had already contacted all the hospitals and the city morgue but nothing; not a word about the disappearance of young Kelly. They tried the British and Irish shipping company for a list of passengers who had travelled to England over the past week but without success; Eddie Kelly's name was not on any list. It was only a week, but if he had been injured, hurt or fell into the river Liffey, good chance he'd have been found by now.

The following night as Brannigan sat sipping his pint in the Flowing Tide public house he suddenly remembered reading something in the Evening Herald the previous week about an American warship coming to Dublin on a visit. He finished his drink in one gulp and headed to his office. Back in the Bridewell he picked up the telephone. "Sergeant," he said, "put me through to the Harbour Master's Office."

The phone rang a couple of times before it was answered by a sleepy voice. "Hello, Harbour Master's Office here. Can I help you?"

"Listen chief. Detective Brannigan, Special Branch. I need to ask you a few questions."

"Yes detective," replied the sleepy voice. "Fire away. Fire away."

"Tell me this; was there a warship, a naval vessel, in Dublin Port last Friday night?" "Yeh there certainly was its all very strange detective, very strange indeed. The USS Neptune, an American warship sailed in last Friday night. It was supposed to stay for a week in Dublin, but you'll never believe this detective; on Saturday morning it was gone, not a sign of it at all, disappeared off the face of the earth. Never even left us in a few bottles of that Yankee gargle; sour mash they call it. Lousy bastards, that's what they are, lousy bastards."

"What do you mean 'disappeared' chief? Where did the ship go?" "That's the funny thing detective. We haven't got a clue. It came in about seven o'clock on the Friday evening and be Jaysus Mister Brannigan, the next morning it was gone. All very strange. We can't make head or tail of it. Why? Is something up detective?" continued the sleepy voice. "Listen chief, will you find out where the ship's going to? What's its destination? And by the way can you give me a call back as soon as you hear something? Thank's chief." Basher put the phone down. *Christ,* he thought, *I figured that this was going to be easy. There's definitely something very funny going on here but I'll solve this little mystery so I will. There has to be some connection with young Kelly's disappearance and the ship, there has to be.* He was absolutely certain and he was seldom wrong.

The ringing of the phone interrupted his thoughts. It was the duty sergeant, "Detective Brannigan, a body has been pulled from the Liffey. It's a young male, long haired, about eighteen years of age, down at Sir John Rogerson's Quay, beside Lime Street."

Brannigan's heart sank.

The voice continued, "But it's just been confirmed, detective; it's not that missing lad from Finglas, Eddie Kelly. It's a student studying Architecture at Bolton Street; a country lad from Limerick city by the name of Pat Deegan, we found his wallet. We think he might have committed suicide because his girlfriend left Ireland and went back to college in America. Her father is an American and works at Shannon airport. The family live in Limerick". Brannigan felt relieved. He put Eddie Kelly to the back of his mind and headed towards the car pool to pick up his police car and drive the short distance to Lime Street. Business as usual for detective Basher Brannigan, sorting out the night time dead of Dublin city.

THE SCOOP

The following Wednesday night the phone rang in the detective's room at the Bridewell. A sleepy voice said, "Detective Brannigan? Harbour Master's office here." Basher had completely forgotten about Eddie Kelly.

"I've got some news for you detective," the sleepy voice continued. "It's that American ship you enquired about. You'll never believe it, Mister Brannigan; we contacted the US Naval Authorities in Norfolk, Virginia and they say the that USS Neptune was never in Dublin and it's visit was cancelled, called away somewhere else, and me seeing the ship with me very own eyes. They won't tell us its destination, so I'm afraid that's the end of the story. Sorry I can't help you, detective. All very strange, so it is. All very strange indeed." The phone went dead. *Christ* thought Basher *there's a lot more to this than meets the eye.* He pondered his next move. With that he picked up the telephone and asked the duty sergeant to get him the American Embassy in Dublin. A cheery American voice answered the phone.

"Detective Brannigan here, Dublin Special Branch. Can I speak to John O'Shay, please?"

"Well well, Detective Brannigan," it was John O'Shay on the line. "How yah doing, buddy, long time no speak."

The two hadn't spoken for almost two years.

"John," said Brannigan, "I need your help, I need a favour. Will you meet me tomorrow at about seven o'clock in the Flowing Tide public house; you know the place in Abbey Street, my local, you know where it is?"

"What's the problem Brannigan?" asked John. "You sound worried."

"Listen, John," replied Brannigan, "I'll give you the full story tomorrow night, I just need you to do a favour for me John."

"Okay Brannigan anything I can do to help, look forward to seeing you tomorrow night detective."

John O'Shay, an official at the American Embassy in Dublin, owed Detective Basher Brannigan a big favour. Some years before, Detective Brannigan was on temporary security duty at the American Embassy in Dublin, standing in for a Special Branch officer who was off with a serious illness. One night O'Shay had returned in the early hours of the morning in the company of a young Dublin lady of the night, both of them the worse for wear. Brannigan should have reported O'Shay for a serious breach of security but he didn't. The two became good friends afterwards but they had lost contact when Brannigan's three-month temporary duty in the embassy was finished.

What Brannigan didn't know was that John O'Shay was not an ordinary embassy employee; he was also a senior C.I.A. official based in the American Embassy in Dublin.

The two met the next night in the Flowing Tide public house in Abbey Street which was situated across the road from the Abbey Theatre and a regular haunt for the Dublin theatre crowd and for the citys' journalists.

After a few pints of Guinness, Brannigan said to O'Shay, "John I need your help with something, I need some information about an American ship."

"What's up?" replied O'Shay, wondering what was on the big cop's mind.

Brannigan told the story of how Eddie Kelly had gone missing and that he was last seen with a black sailor. He even told him about Eddie's brother Paddy Kelly and how he was killed in Africa. He told O'Shea how he thought the disappearance of young man might be related to the American ship. He wanted to know why the American Naval Authorities denied that the ship had been in Dublin.

O'Shay began to laugh. "Christ, Brannigan," he said. "Your suspicious detective's mind is working overtime. You've got this one totally wrong Basher. I'm surprised at you detective you must be losing that magic touch in your old age. You're totally wrong, you're barking up the wrong tree. There's nothing mysterious about the USS Neptune, Brannigan," O'Shea continued. "The ship docked in Dublin last Friday night but was ordered to pull anchor, ordered to sail to Vietnam. We're at war Brannigan. The United States is at war with the Vietcong. I was at an official dinner at the American Embassy with the ship's Captain – Captain William Grant and his officers – the night the ship was in Dublin? Listen, Brannigan I can assure you that the ship and the young lad's disappearance are in no way connected with the USS Neptune, no way at all. The Naval Authorities probably denied it was in Dublin for security reasons. The United States is at war with the Communists. It's understandable Brannigan, don't you agree?"

"But O'Shea," Brannigan interrupted. "Kelly was last seen with a black sailor, and it had to be an American sailor. I've checked. There were only a couple of merchant ships in Dublin Port that night and the merchant seamen don't wear uniforms, do yeh get my drift. There has to be some connection with the uniformed sailor. There has to be, I'm certain of it so I am. The young fella didn't just disappear off the face of the earth, now did he, there's no trace of him, we would have found a body by now."

"Listen," said O'Shea, "if, and only if, Kelly was on the ship, which I doubt, it's strictly forbidden to bring civilians on board an American naval vessel, the night watch would never have allowed it, the captain would have informed Naval Headquarters by now and they would have notified the Irish Authorities. That's naval regulations Brannigan," he continued, "I think you're jumping to conclusions on this one. You've just got it all wrong this time, putting one and one together and getting three. But I'll tell you what I'll do; I'll contact the ship by radio and speak to Captain Grant directly – he's actually a very decent guy. His family come from Ireland you know; from up the north somewhere– just to confirm that Kelly is not on the ship. Okay, Brannigan?"

"Thanks John. I appreciate your help," replied Brannigan as he drank the heel of his pint, still not fully convinced by what O'Shea had said. He was still certain that there was some connection between Eddie Kelly's disappearance and the American warship.

While Brannigan and O'Shea were deep in discussion, a well-known Dublin journalist called Nosey McDowell had been watching the pair trying to overhear their conversation. He knew them both and he clocked that something was up. His years of practice as a journalist gave him a nose for a story; that's how he earned his nickname. He picked up snatches of the conversation; something about a missing Dublin lad Eddie Kelly from Finglas an undertaker's assistant with Shaky Shanahan; Brannigan mentioned a black fella been seen with Kelly before he disappeared. Something about the young fella Kelly's brother being killed in the Irish Army in Africa. He remembered the case years ago; the Irish Army were in Katanga on a peacekeeping mission with the United Nations and Irish soldiers were killed by the blacks. What did yeh called them? They had a funny sort of name. Yeh, the Balubas. Now young Kelly disappears, last seen with a black fella – all very strange. His heart raced. What a scoop for tomorrow's paper. But why, he wondered, was O'Shea involved? He'd heard rumours about O'Shea. *Fuck it!* He thought. *There's a story in this one alright.*

He finished his drink and headed back to his office in Abbey Street. He pulled out all the back editions of the newspaper and within an hour had the entire press cuttings on the Katanga Massacre over in the Congo on his desk. Then he found what he was looking for. On the front page of a back edition: the story all about the death of Private First Class Patrick Christopher Kelly with a faded black and white photograph of a handsome smiling young soldier in battle fatigues, Lee Enfield rifle in hand. The article also contained the family address in Finglas.

He rushed down the stairs and jumped into a taxi in O'Connell's Street. Twenty minute's later; he knocked loudly on the Kelly's front door. Seamy opened the door.

"Whatever you're bleedin selling mister we don't want any so fuck off. Do yeh hear me now scarper." the door slammed shut in Nosey's face.

Nosey knocked again. "No Mister Kelly you don't understand, I'm not selling anything, It's about your missing son Eddie, he has gone missing hasn't he?"

The front door opened.

"Yeh the little bleeder's gone missin all right so he has. He's fucked off to England over to dat pal of his, the big lanky Monks fucker, leaving his mother and me here to starve to death. Destitute, dat's what we are, bleedin mister destitute, all because of that little good for nuthin selfish bastard.When I get me hands on the little fecker, I'll ring his fuckin neck so I will. Anyway what the fuck is it to you?" Seamy was slightly puzzled.

"McDowell is the name. I'm a journalist with the Evening Herald; I want to talk to you about your son Eddie."

"I bleedin well told you all you need to know. He's a fuckin waster, a bleedin ungrateful little fucker. When I get me bleedin hands on the bastard he's fuckin dead so he is."

"Do you know about the black fella Mister Kelly?"

"What bleedin black fella are you talking about?"

"He was last seen with a black fella, they think it might have something to do with his disappearance so they do. He might have been kidnapped or killed him or even worse."

"Ah go on outa dat will yeh, what the fuck are yeh talkin about? The little bleeder has fucked off to England, over to dat Monks fella, and dat's the end of the story so it is."

"No Mister Kelly dat's where you're wrong so yeh are. Listen to what I'm saying now Mister Kelly; dat's not the story. The story is that a black fella may have kidnapped him or worse."

"Jaysus mister answer me this if yeh can. First they kill me son Paddy, dem black bastards, and now you're saying they've come all the way over here to Dublin from the Congo and taken me son Eddie too. But Jaysus how the fuck did the Balubas know where we live? And tell me this if yeh can mister, how did the black fucker's recognise Eddie, now answer me dat if yeh can?"

The next evening on his way to work, Detective Brannigan called into the Flowing Tide. Every evening he'd walk from his lodgings in Drumcondra to the city centre and call in to his favourite bar, have a few pints of Guinness, and read the newspaper before commencing the dead shift at the Bridewell. He couldn't believe his eyes when he opened the early edition of the Evening Herald.

The headlines read:

YOUNG DUBLINER MISSING.LAST SEEN WITH BLACK MAN!

The article gave scant details about Eddie's disappearance, just a couple of lines, but half the front page was the full story of Paddy's death in the Congo and a photograph of Paddy in his army uniform was printed above the article. The article faintly suggested that there was some connection between Eddie's disappearance and Paddy's murder by the Balubas in the Congo.

Brannigan couldn't believe what he was reading. *Christ,* he thought, *how in God's name did the Herald find out about the disappearance of Eddie Kelly?*

It was Sergeant Molloy who showed Bridie the newspaper when she called into the Garda station, as she did every day after her visit to the church. She nearly fainted when she saw Paddy's photograph and read the headlines. It brought back all the pain of Paddy's death; that terrible night when the young army dispatch rider brought her the dreadful news. She struggled to control her tears. "What does it all mean sergeant?" she asked. "I don't understand. You mean the Balubas have taken me two sons? What did we ever do on the Balubas? At school my boy's used to give all their pennies to the black babies? I just don't understand sergeant," said Bridie. "What have we ever done to deserve this? Anyway how did the Balubas recognise Eddie, how did they find out where we live? I just don't understand any of it at all."

Sergeant Molloy didn't understand either. He was totally perplexed, how did the Balubas recognise Eddie?

Bridie was in hysterics, she wept uncontrollably. All Sergeant Molloy could do was take her out to the squad car and drive her the short distance to her home. But she got worse and worse, screaming and shouting blaming Seamy for everything. It got so bad that Seamy had to ask Mary O'Toole to go down to the village and get Doctor Flanagan to come up to see Bridie. The doctor prescribed a strong sedative and Bridie went to bed.

During her long rest in bed Bridie had only two visitors Mary O' Toole who called almost every day and Colette Murphy. The Friday night he went missing Colette had waited patiently all night in the Go-Go club for Eddie to arrive with his drunken swagger and his corny jokes and the way he'd hug her and drag her wildly around the dance floor.

"Any chance of a ride tonight?" he'd always ask.

And she always replied, "No chance yeh dirty bastard."

But this time it would be different, she would answer, "Yes of course me darling Eddie. You can pull down my knickers and ride me anytime you like."

She couldn't wait to see the look on his face; he'd die of shock so he would. She shivered with excitement just thinking about it. She stood with Imelda and Mickser near the entrance door of the Go-Go club chain smoking and waiting patiently all night, waiting for Eddie to arrive, to see his smiling face.

Every Friday night when he came into the club he always stood out from the rest of the crowd. There was something about her Eddie; he was so vibrant, always the centre of attraction and that's why he was so special. But that night he never came. She was heartbroken. Anto O'Toole told her that Eddie had run off to England but she didn't believe him. She knew Eddie would never run off and leave her no, not without saying something first. She knew Eddie loved her.

One evening when she got home from work, her father showed her the article in the Evening Herald about Eddie's disappearance. She nearly died with shock. She could only think of one thing to do. She asked her brother Tommy to give her a lift up to Finglas on his Honda motorbike. When she arrived at the Kelly house, Seamy took her up to Bridie's bedroom. She was shocked at the state of Bridie who she had meet once when she was in town with Eddie one Saturday afternoon buying him new clothes in Arnott's Department Store in Henry Street. Bridie looked like an old woman; she was in a terrible state.

Colette sat beside Bridie on the bed. "Missus Kelly, how are yeh? I came to find out about your Eddie. What's all this in the Herald about him been kidnapped and maybe murdered? It's not true is it, Missus Kelly? It's not true?" she said, tear's streaming down her cheeks. "I don't know, answered Bridie, putting her arms around Colette. "I just don't know any more me nerves are wrecked with worry so they are. I just don't know where to turn." "Listen, Missus Kelly you're not to worry everything will be alright I promise yeh Eddie will be home soon safe and sound I just know he will. I promise yeh so I do. Eddie would never desert us like this. He'll be home soon I just know he will Missus Kelly. I just know he will.

BUDDHIST PHILOSOPHY

S ergeant Molloy took great pity on Bridie Kelly. He had to do something to help her but what could he possibly do for the poor woman? He picked up the telephone and rang every Garda station in Dublin City to see if he could find out something about the disappearance of Eddie Kelly and the source of the newspaper article. But nothing, not a word; none of the Garda station's knew anything about the missing lad or how the story got into the newspaper. He finally rang the offices of the Evening Herald and spoke to Nosey McDowell.

"Mister McDowell," Sergeant Molloy enquired, "the story in today's Herald; where the hell did you get your information from and how do you know a black fella abducted young Kelly? Why has this information not been reported to the Garda? It's all a pack of lies, all made up just to sell newspapers, isn't it, McDowell? You just print any old story and be damned as long as it sells papers; no consideration for the damage or hurt it causes". The sergeant continued. "If you could see the state Eddie Kelly's mother is in you'd be ashamed of yourself. The poor woman is in a terrible way and it's entirely your fault. Christ, when she saw that photo of her son Paddy on the front page of the Herald all the pain came flooding back the poor woman nearly died of a heart attack."

After a moment's silence Nosey replied. "Hold on a minute now Sergeant Molloy. I think you've got the wrong end of the stick here everything I printed is true, well, almost true. And by the way I never said the Kelly fella was abducted; I just said he was missing, last seen with a black fella and may have been abducted.

Get your facts right sergeant."But who gave you this information Mister Mc Dowell".

"Let's just say that one of your own has a very big mouth so he has"

"What do yeh mean by that Mc Dowell?" "Why don't you ask that big gorilla Brannigan in the Special Branch he'll know what I'm talkin about so he will?"

He slammed the phone down on Sergeant Molloy.

Later that evening he rang the Bridewell and asked to speak to Detective Brannigan. "Sergeant Molloy here," he said, "Finglas Garda station. "It's about this young missing lad from Finglas, Eddie Kelly. His mother Bridie reported him missing a couple of weeks ago and I reported the case to headquarters. His mother she's in a terrible state. Did you see the Herald today and the article about young Kelly, and all the stuff about the brother who was killed in the army? Jaysus are yeh trying to kill the poor woman or what? Hasn't she suffered enough, the poor creature?"

"I saw the article all right?" replied Brannigan, slightly taken aback by the sergeant's outburst. "It's all a pack of lies; I don't know where they got their information from."

"Well I can tell you the answer to that one so I can," replied Sergeant Molloy. "It came from you Mr Brannigan."

"What do you mean sergeant?" replied Brannigan angrily.

Nosey McDowell, the reporter from the Evening Herald overheard your conversation regarding Eddie Kelly in the pub detective?" continued Sergeant Molloy.

Brannigan was dumbfounded, then it dawned on him. McDowell was in the Flowing Tide the night he met John O'Shay from the American Embassy. He remembered seeing McDowell lurking in the background, sneaking around like a thief in the night but he hadn't taken much notice of him. The bastard was eavesdropping on the conversation.

"Look Sergeant Molloy," said Brannigan, "I never told Nosey McDowell anything about this case and that's a fact. I was following an unofficial line of enquiry about the young lad and I was talking about the disappearance to one of my contacts in a pub the other night, McDowell was there and must have overheard the conversation."

"Is Eddie Kelly dead detective?" asked Sergeant Molloy.

"I don't believe so," replied Brannigan.

"But where is the young lad and what's all this about a black fella? What does it all mean? His mother nearly died of shock when she saw the article in the paper and the picture of her son Paddy. The eldest son Paddy was killed by Balubas. You know the story detective."

"Yes I know all about it," replied Brannigan. "Look," he continued. "Look sergeant, I'm following an unofficial line of enquiry about the young lad and I have a hunch where he might be."

Sergeant Molloy listened in amazement. "You mean he's definitely still alive detective?"

"I didn't say that," replied Brannigan. "But I am following a definite lead, which may turn up something. Forget about all that nonsense in the newspaper."

"Can I tell his mother?" replied Sergeant Molloy. "Can I tell her there's some hope of her son coming home?"

"No," replied Brannigan curtly. "No, don't say anything yet. Look Sergeant Molloy I can tell you're very concerned about Missus Kelly. I'll tell you what; as soon as something turns up I promise I'll give you a ring. If I find out where he is I'll let you know immediately and you can tell his mother. In the meantime, say nothing. I'm only at the early stage of my enquiries so I am and I may be barking up the wrong tree."

Sergeant Molloy felt good. His first impulse was to jump in the squad car, drive up to Bridies house and tell her he had some news, some hope, that Eddie was still alive. *Yes, he thought, I've got a good feeling that everything will turn out fine and poor Bridie Kelly will get her son Eddie home soon safe and sound.*

Sergeant Molloy had one more thing to do with regard to Eddie Kelly; he picked up the telephone and contacted the parochial house in Saint Canice's church. There was a church mission in Finglas village being run by the Jesuit priests and, while he knew that he couldn't say anything to Bridie about his conversation with Brannigan to give her hope, the second best thing was to ask one of the mission priests to call at her house and speak to her and give her some comfort for he knew she was a deeply religious woman.

Later that evening, Father Michael O'Donohue, a young Jesuit priest from Cork who was running the mission in Saint Canice's Church, sat beside Bridie's bed and tried to console her. It was Father O'Donohues first mission after finishing his theology degree in Rome. He listened patiently to the story of her family and began to understand her deep sense of grief and loss. He tried to console the grieving woman, but he just couldn't think of the right words to say to help her.

"Father," she asked with a solemn voice, "what have I ever done to deserve this? My father was shot by the English then my first-born son was eaten by the Balubas and now me only remaining son Eddie is gone missing. Father what am I going to do? What have I ever done to deserve all this suffering?" Bridie continued. "The suffering me own mother went through, Father. She died of a broken heart so she did. Tell me Father, why is God so cruel to us poor unfortunate Irish mothers?"

Young Father O'Donohue felt a tear in his eye, he remembered his own mother on her death bed dying of cancer and her crying in pain and how she suffered dreadfully before she died. He could not answer the poor woman's questions, he just couldn't think of any words to console her or to ease her pain.

"Missus Kelly," he said, "I'll say a prayer at the mass tonight for the safe return of your son and everything will be all right. Your son will come home safe and sound I'm sure of it." But the young priest wasn't convinced by his own words. He felt a sense of relief as he left the Kelly household and headed towards Finglas village and St. Canice's Church. As he walked to the church he tried to use his rational mind to come to terms with all that had happened to this unfortunate woman: Her father, then her sons and on top of that she gets married to a drunken layabout; and the dreadful state of the house and that awful pervading smell of pig's feet, it turned his stomach. Why are some families cursed? He wondered, are these tragedies inevitable? Does this poor woman bring all this misfortune on herself? Was her father evil for taking up arms and trying to kill English soldiers? where did it get him killed, leaving a wife and two children. The grief and pain of her father's death must have affected the whole family even carrying on to this very day. This unfortunate woman has never recovered from the terrible loss; it affected her whole life and her family somehow. Her eldest son Paddy killed and now Eddie missing. Maybe she's created the situation herself; do we create our own hell or heaven on this earth? He'd read about that concept somewhere, the *Law of Attraction or the Law of Resonance*. If you think good thoughts, good things can happen or vice versa. Wasn't that some form of Buddhist philosophy? Young Father O'Donohue had no answers and his honours degree in Theology didn't help. As he entered Saint Canice's Church he thought to himself, *I'll say a special prayer for Bridie Kelly tonight at Mass for the safe return of her son and for God's grace to help her find peace of mind.*

John O'Shea, at the American Embassy finally contacted Detective Brannigan a couple of days later.

"Brannigan," he said, "I've contacted the United States naval headquarters at Virginia. I couldn't speak directly to the Neptune; however the Naval Authorities inform me that a stowaway was not reported on the ship. Brannigan Kelly is definitely not on the Neptune. So detective that's that. I'm afraid I can't help you and as I said before detective there's no way a civilian would ever get onboard an American Naval vessel, impossible. By the way," continued O'Shea, "any word yet about the disappearance of the young lad? I saw that article in the Evening Herald?"

"No," replied Brannigan with disappointment in his voice. "We've no word about Kelly's disappearance nothing at all."

"Sorry I can't help detective and by the way if you find Eddie Kelly don't forget to let me know". The phone went dead.

As Brannigan sat in the darkness slowly sipping a Powers whiskey he felt bitterly disappointed. All along he was so sure that young Kelly was on that American ship. He was seldom wrong. But anyway it was all over now, there was nothing else he could do; on this occasion he was wrong. Maybe Eddie Kelly had run off to England.

THE OLD COUNTRY

Captain William Grant paced uneasily up and down the bridge of the USS Neptune in his crisp, starched, white naval uniform. He was a worried man. His troubles had begun the night he arrived in Ireland: a place he had wanted to visit all his life. His great grandfather had emigrated to America from Ireland during the potato famine of 1847 so a visit to the old country was something he had looked forward to since he was a child, listening to his grandmother telling stories about Ireland. He had intended to hire a car in Dublin and drive to where his family had originated from: a place called Buncrana somewhere in County Donegal; somewhere in the north of the country in Ulster. Black 47 it was called and the Grant family were starving. The potato crop, their main food source, had failed for a second year. In desperation the family went to the local priest for help. They never got to see the priest. Huddled crowds of starving people were gathered outside the priest's house begging for food; hordes of crying women and children, the men standing silent, looking at the snow-covered ground utterly helpless; women wailing, clutching starving babies to their breasts. The priest had given all he had. There was nothing left and even he was feeling the pangs of hunger. What could they do? In total desperation to try and get some food, the Grant family went to the house of the local protestant minister. The minister told them that if they converted to the protestant faith he would feed them. But they refused to become 'Soupers', a name given to Catholic's who, for a bowl of soup, converted to Protestantism.

Sell their sowl's for penny rowls,
And soup and hairy bacon

But they would never abandon the faith of their forefathers: the faith that had given them succour throughout all the years of desperation and English oppression. They would rather die than take the soup, and they did, all except Captain Grant's great grandfather. The family huddled together in the bleak thatched roofed stone cabin that was to become their grave and on a freezing cold winter's night they, one by one, lapsed into the sweet sleep of unconsciousness and died peacefully. But the youngest boy was strong. His mother had secretly given him what little food they had from their meagre store of corn, and that had kept him alive. She knew they were dying; he had to survive, to escape and to live. He struggled from the cottage that was his family's tomb. With great effort, on the dying embers of the turf fire, he lit some straw from their bedding and set alight the dry thatch under the eaves. As he stumbled in the blinding snow he stopped for a moment and looked back at the burning cottage that was the funeral pyre of his family. His whole life was gone in the whirling, dull, grey smoke billowing skyward from the burning thatched roof.

He then started the long walk to Derry City, which was about twelve miles from Buncrana; it was his only chance. He knew the hunger hadn't reached the city and he might get some food there so he staggered along in the snow, kept going by a deep force: the desire to survive. An hour later overcome by hunger and exhaustion he collapsed on the side of the road. That should have been the end of him, but a short time later a large horse drawn open cart, owned by the local landlord , picked him up from the side of the road. He was fortunate. The famine had given the landlord a perfect excuse to remove the tenants from his land so he agreed to pay their fare to America if they deserted their farms. It was their only chance to escape the hunger and certain death-they had no choice.

The cart was taking the tenants to Derry to board a ship bound for Boston and that was how Captain Grant's great grandfather escaped from the hunger and misery of his native land and survived. Grant knew the story so very well.

He was curious to visit Buncrana, and see the home of his ancestors. But that all changed on his first night in Dublin. He had enjoyed the party at the American Embassy the Guinness and Irish dancing, a great night and a great start to his expected one week's holiday in Ireland. O'Shea at the embassy had treated him so graciously. However, that all changed in the early hours of the following morning. At four a.m. the officer of the watch woke him; it was a signal from Naval Headquarters in Norfolk, Virginia. The United States of America was at war. North Vietnamese gunships had torpedoed an American destroyer in the Mekong Delta and Captain Grant was ordered to pull anchor immediately and sail at full speed on a war footing to Vietnam.

His visit to Donegal had to be postponed. But things got worse. A couple of hour's later, Peters found a stowaway on the ship: a young guy, a bloody long haired Dublin hippie. A stowaway on a warship was unheard of. This could seriously damage his career in the navy.

Okay the guy was now in the brig; the crew didn't know he was on the ship apart from Peters and the watch sailors. That's okay but the ship was due to dock in Saigon docks in about five weeks, how could he get the stowaway back to Ireland without a trace without a paper trail? He had to figure that one out but he had a contact in Saigon who might be able to help.

It was the boom, boom, boom, thumping noise that awoke the sleeping Eddie Kelly from his drunken stupor, as he lay sleeping on the cold metal floor of the warship with a smile on his face. It was the deep hypnotic metallic sound resonating in his head. Boom! Boom! Boom! It had carried him along on a soft rhythmical wave of sleep. He opened his eyes in almost complete darkness and for a few seconds he didn't know where he was. He was confused. His head was fuzzy. Christ what a hangover, what a night. Then it started to come back to him. Jaysus he hadn't really sang that stupid rebel song, James Connolly, had he? God he must have been drunk. But what a bloody good night. Brilliant, absolutely brilliant! The boom, boom, boom reminded him of something, but what? What was it? Then he remembered it was a long time ago. He could see it all vividly now; early on a Saturday morning; the Isle of Man steam packet boat. They were all going on a day trip to the

Isle of Man sailing from Dublin Port to Douglas. They were all there: his ma and pa, him and Paddy. Paddy wore his army uniform. It was the first time he wore his uniform in public and he was so proud. Bridie was so proud of her son. Eddie was so proud of his brother. Seamy was delighted – some money coming in at last.

Paddy had organised and paid for the trip and given his father some spending money.

That lovely day so long ago; they were so happy then; the funny accent of the Manx people; the cats with no tails. As soon as they arrived they took a trip on the electric railway up to see the Laxey wheel near Cooil Roi, the three of them laughing and joking all except Seamy. Seamy had a few pounds and he wanted to drink it. He searched all the bars on the waterfront but he couldn't find a single moocher. All the bars were empty. He walked up Prospect Hill and entered the Duke of York public house – not a moocher in sight. He settled in supping pint after pint of watery bitter and trying to engage in conversation with the odd local without much success. Nobody laughed at his jokes except the young barmaid. She was from Liverpool but her parent's were originally from Dublin. Seamy spent the day chatting her up; not a bad little thing; gamey enough; nice little arse.

"Boring bleedin kip this Isle of Man. No crack at all," Seamy muttered to himself as he staggered down the hill towards the port, half-drunk just about in time to catch the boat back to Dublin and his fellow moochers.

Yes it was the noise of a ship's engine. Boom! Boom! Boom! Yes, that's it. Eddie got it now. It was the sound of a ship's engine ploughing through the waves. A ship moving through the waves? The reality hit him with a bang. He jumped up quickly hitting his head on the low metal ceiling. As he pushed open the door and stepped into the galley he bumped straight into First Officer Peters.

"Holy Moses who the hell are you, mister?" Peters was shocked at the sight of the dishevelled Eddie with his long hair, round glasses, crumpled clothes and reeking of alcohol. "What the hell are you doing on this ship mister? Christ, I don't believe it – a God-damned stowaway. Wait till the captain finds out. You're in big trouble mister, big big trouble."

He grabbed Eddie roughly by the arm and led him directly to the bridge.

Captain Grant couldn't believe his bad luck. A stowaway on a naval vessel. His heart sank. After twenty-five years of a totally unblemished record he had an unwanted civilian aboard when they were on full war alert. It was unthinkable to have a stowaway; it showed a serious lack of security. He knew he would be in big trouble with his superiors. This incident would seriously damage his chances of commanding a bigger ship. His life-long ambition to become an admiral was in jeopardy. He considered the situation carefully, his long years in command had taught him that every problem had a solution. He had to keep his cool, consider the situation very carefully and look at every option. He knew that it was imperative to keep the stowaway a secret. He could not inform his superiors. The situation must be kept under control. As soon as they reached their destination, he would have to get this guy off the ship and home with as little fuss as possible. There was always a way.

Eddie was taken down to the brig before the ship came alive. After several hours of questioning the young Irishman the captain felt more confident. He believed Eddie's story that he had had met a lone black sailor who brought him aboard the ship. He knew the culprit would be one of the black sailors – always untrustworthy – and his thoughts turned to retribution, when he found the sailor who was responsible for bringing a civilian onboard his ship he would make him pay.

The stowaway was from a poor Dublin family with no connections. He was sure nobody knew Eddie had come aboard his ship, he would never be missed and when he returned home to Ireland no one would believe his story. The captain had it all worked out; he would keep the young guy confined to the brig and get him off the Neptune as quietly as possible as soon as they had docked in Saigon. No one would be the wiser and he could still make admiral. No paperwork that was the key; no paper trail. The plan was good.

He turned to the first officer. "Listen and listen good Peters; I want this kept quiet and I want nobody onboard to know this guy is here, keep him in solitary confinement Peters don't foul up on this one, keep this under wraps and I may just approve your application for promotion."

The captain looked at Eddie with total contempt in his face.

"Listen son I can't get you off this ship till we reach our destination in about five week's time. We're on radio silence," the captain lied, "so I cannot inform the Irish authorities that you're onboard. As soon as we reach port I will get you back home."

Eddie could not believe what he was hearing. "What am I going to do captain? What about me ma and me job? Me ma will die of worry so she will. Ah Jaysus captain you have got to get me home. I'm the only one working in me house so I am, what will me ma and da do for food, they won't be able to pay the rent. I look after them. They'll starve to death, so they will." There was desperation in Eddie's voice. He began to cry.

The captain replied angrily, "Listen mister and listen well; I want to tell you something. This is my ship and I don't want you here so shut up. You had no right coming aboard this ship. Do you hear me now son? When we dock I will get you home and that's the end of the story."

As they both left the brig the captain suddenly stopped and turned around to Eddie. "Hold on a minute son." he said. "I believe there may be a way out of this God-damn awful mess. We're due to meet a supply ship off the coast of England in two days time. I could get you off the Neptune then, the supply ship could drop you off in Liverpool in the United Kingdom; it's an easy trip to Dublin from there, you could be back home in a couple of days."

Peters was puzzled. He knew there was no supply ship. What was the captain playing at?

"Jaysus captain dat's fantastic news so it is. Thank you, thank you, sir." Eddie jumped up and threw his arms around Captain Grant.

"Okay buddy," said the captain, a sarcastic smile on his face. "But there's just one little thing you have to do for me first just one little thing."

"Anything captain," replied Eddie pure relief in his voice. "Anything at all, just let me get home, sir."

"Okay all you have to do is tell me the name of the sailor who brought you aboard my ship."

Eddie felt his heart sink. He wanted home badly more than anything else in the whole world. He was so desperate. He thought for a moment. *Why shouldn't he tell the captain about Jerome? It was his fault anyway. If Jerome hadn't come into his pub on his big night he wouldn't be on the ship. It was his entire fault for bringing him aboard the Neptune.* But Eddie Kelly was no grass. He liked the black sailors; they were good to him and he knew Jerome would be in serious trouble if he named him. He remembered his mothers' stories about informers and what happened to them. He remembered the story about the postman Matt Corrigan and his grandfather Christy. He thought for a second about the Mauser pistol in Paddy's bedroom. He imagined Major Morley standing there in his English officer's uniform just like the captain. No he couldn't do it, Eddie Kelly was no informer.

"I'm sorry captain; I don't know his name, I just can't remember sir; I was drunk at the time so I was. I want to go home more than anything else in the whole world but I honestly can't remember his name. All I know is that he was black and all the black faces look the same to me so they do captain."

The captain knew he was lying. Not as stupid as he looks the Irish hippie. He turned abruptly and left the cell with Peters leaving Eddie sitting alone on the metal bunk. As the heavy door slammed tears began to stream down Eddie's face. He trembled with fear.

Captain Grant felt confident he had the situation under control. Okay the Irish guy hadn't named the sailor who brought him onboard the ship but he knew it must have been one of the twenty or so black sailor's who went on shore-leave the night before. He would bide his time. There were ways and means; he would find out the name sooner or later. He questioned the night watch although he knew he would find out nothing; it was too serious a charge. Anyway, it was no longer a problem; that ass-licking idiot Peters would handle everything. So he put the stowaway to the back of his mind. He had more important matters to deal with, as his ship sailed on its long journey towards Vietnam and the conflict in South East Asia.

Peters had to confide in the two leading seamen who were responsible for security of the brig. He briefed the two seamen with strict orders to keep the stowaway a secret from the rest of the crew. Nobody was to know Eddie Kelly was onboard the ship but the captain was right – Peters was an idiot.

One of the leading seamen was Sonny, Jerome's best friend who had let him bring Eddie onboard the ship. As soon as Peters left Sonny was straight to the brig and Eddie told him the whole story. He quickly realised that the young Irish guy had not named Jerome to the captain. They owed him a big favour; he hadn't squealed not even to get home. Later that day when Sonny told Jerome what had happened he was shocked. He felt so guilty. *Christ it was all his fault*, he thought. *Why the hell had he brought the Irish guy onboard the ship?* How could he have been so stupid? He would have been dishonourably discharged from the navy and sent straight to the State Penitentiary. Jesus, it would have killed his folk's back home in Detroit – no more money sent home every month to help feed the young family. Jerome was the oldest child in his family and all his young brother's and sister's adored him. *Christ*, he thought, *I could really have messed things up. Thank god that the young Irish guy kept quiet and told the captain nothing. Christ, the disgrace to his mum and pop.* He couldn't bear to think about it.

At the first opportunity Jerome rushed to the brig to see his Irish hero Eddie Kelly. He hugged Eddie. "Eddie, Eddie he said "how can I thank you for what you've done for me and the rest of the guys. I'll be forever grateful to you Eddie I love you buddy, I love you like a brother". Eddie started to cry. "Jerome I couldn't betray you and Sonny and the rest of the sailors. How could I, yis were all so good to me so yis were, I know all about squealers so I do. I would never betray my friend's never". "Eddie we'll get you home bro don't you worry about a thing everything will work out just fine." "Jerome can I ask yeh a question "Eddie had a serious expression on his face "Of course Eddie what's on your mind"? The captain said we were going to Vietnam, is that near France Jerome"? Eddie was never good at geography at school. "No brother don't you know nuthin, it's in South East Asia that's where we're fighting the war". "What war" asked Eddie? "The war against the commies" replied Jerome, "the little fucker's that are trying to take over the free world". Eddie looked confused."Who's fighting the war"? "We are Eddie, its Uncle Sam's war".

"Who's Uncle Sam Jerome"? "Jesus Eddie, are you plain dumb, I can't believe you never heard of Uncle Sam, the United States of America, but don't you worry Eddie it's not your war brother you're going home". "Thank fuck" replied Eddie, I don't want to be in any wars, me granddad and me big brother were killed in wars. No Jerome, I just want to go home to Dublin and me job as an undertaker's assistant".

When Jerome told everything to the sailors who had been drinking with Eddie the night before he became their hero their Irish rebel hero. He had saved Jerome and probably Sonny from a dishonourable discharge from the navy, also he never mentioned the sailors drinking on the ship. They decided that they would do everything they possibly could to look after Eddie until he got home and to make his stay in the brig of the Neptune as comfortable as they could. They spent as much time as possible with him to keep him company. They would play cards and tell him all about the States; anything just to pass the time and keep him from getting home sick. Eddie got an ample supply of Playboy magazines, beer, candy and cigarettes, just about anything he wanted. But it was the food that Eddie loved most of all. He had never had so much food before: hamburgers, hot dogs and pretzels. O'Brien, the ship's cook made sure of that. At home there was never enough food in the Kelly house and Eddie always had a hunger. Dinner most evenings was coddle, tripe and cow heel, with fish and chips every Friday on pay day but not always. Some nights Eddie came home to a bare table and a grumbling stomach. He was often reduced to chewing cold pig's feet, if there was any left. Life was hard in the Kelly house but life wasn't hard for Eddie on board the USS Neptune. He began to enjoy the company of the young sailors. He began to learn the walk and talk the talk of the brothers and after a while he could talk the talk and walk the walk. But the American food; hamburgers were his favourite – even better than the ray and chips from Moroney's fish and chip shop back home.

Slowly the day's slipped by and with each passing day the ship came nearer to dry land and the return home to Ireland of the accidental stowaway Eddie Kelly.

Eventually the novelty of self-abuse, leering at the centrefold of Playboy magazine, began to wear off. Each night he went to sleep dreaming about his home. He missed his ma terribly; Shaky and Colette Murphy and his best mate Anto O Toole. Not one night passed that he didn't cry himself to sleep. Then out of the blue he woke up one morning and knew something big was up. He looked out of the porthole and saw land; he could feel the excitement in the air.

As he climbed out of his bunk Jerome and Sonny came running into the brig and Jerome shouted excitedly, "Eddie! It's all over buddy. It's all over, we've reached Vietnam. It's all over. He hugged Eddie. "Eddie it's all over for you now brother you'll be safely back home in Ireland in a couple of days it's all over for you bro.

THE HITLER YOUTH

Master Sergeant Freddie Rock was having a bad day, a very bad day indeed. His gut hurt. He'd drunk too much again last night in the sergeant's mess – too much sour mash. Christ he hated this God-forsaken dump. He'd served in the Second World War and had been with the first wave of marines on the Normandy beaches on D-Day in1944. He'd served in Korea in the fifties, but this; Jesus this was a different sort of war. Those little slanty eyed commie bastards wouldn't stand up and fight like soldiers; hiding in the jungle; hit and run; never showing their ugly yellow faces; just pop up now and then and murder some pimply faced, greenhorn, stateside kid only out of his mother's nappies. Jesus, he hated this place. This wasn't war. These little yellow bastards made him like the Germans. At least they had the gut's to stand up and fight like God-damn men, or boys for that matter, he laughed to himself. It happened well over twenty years ago but he still remembered it as if it was yesterday. Rock was a private in the marines and on flank duty one day as his company was entering a small German village called Frankfurt Am Main, near the border with Luxembourg. Suddenly, from behind some trees, a German soldier fired a panzerfaust grenade launcher, which missed, at the Sherman Tank, which was leading the company into the village. Rock, who was very close to the firing position of the German soldier, ran over anxious to get a kill and see if he could get his hands on a few souvenirs perhaps even the coveted Luger pistol. He was astonished to find that the German soldier, who had fired the grenade launcher, was in fact a young boy of about twelve or thirteen years old dressed in a baggy grey uniform of the Hitler Youth who had been sent out to defend his village by the local Gauleiter.

The terrified boy, who had pissed himself, was shaking with fear and was crying, "Kaput! Kaput!" his hands in the air. Rock blew his head clean off with a single rifle shot fired at point blank range. Christ he was shocked at the devastating effect of the M16 bullet. He had altered the lead cone of the full metal jacket round by drilling a small hole in the tip of the bullet in order that it would explode on contact and it sure did.

He rifled through the dead boy's pockets looking for something of value. All he found was a German Army issue ration pack containing sweets and chocolate. The Hitler Youth got an issue of sweets and chocolate before battle, the men tobacco and Schnapps.

One less Nazi, he thought as he turned and walked away, eating the chocolate and smiling.

Later that day, Rock did feel slightly guilty, when as the company rested in the captured village square and an old woman dressed in black struggled to pull a wooden cart along the cobbled street of the village. The headless body of the dead boy soldier was hanging limply from the cart.

Anyway, thought Rock, putting the German boy to the back of his mind, *these yellow little bastards, shoot and run.* Jesus, he had enough of this shit-hole. He wanted out and that was exactly what he was going to do.

Three months before he had applied to marine headquarters for permission to retire from the army. His application had been approved, he was cashing in. It was payback time for Uncle Sam. He was going home, stateside: full military discharge; clean sheet; no black marks (well, almost none); he was always just about too smart to get on a charge; always one step ahead of them God-damn officers; although, the last charge nearly ruined him. He'd been formally disciplined just weeks before for dereliction of duty after three prisoners escaped from his compound. He was warned by his superiors that the next charge would result in his dishonourable discharge with loss of pension and all accrued benefits so he had to be on his best behaviour at least for a few more weeks. Jesus he hated those fucking officers, all spit and polish. But he'd won his war and now the booty was all his. He'd retire on a pension of half pay for the rest of his life with a nice long service bonus thrown in. He knew exactly what he was going to do: buy a little ranch down south in some little hick town in Alabama or Louisiana. He would sit in the bar every night and tell those civilians all about his heroic exploits, all those long years serving Uncle Sam. Yeh pick up a nice young thing to keep him warm at night.

He looked out over the dusty compound at the line of shiny trucks ready to take the new troops fresh from the States to their posts up country, to fight for the free world against the communists. That was his job: port dispatcher; bring them in and ship them out. All he had to do was get them out to the combat zone. Anyway his papers had just come through. He was going home in a couple of weeks. He would sit at home in the States watching it all on television. Yeh he would buy one of them big fancy televisions like the one in the officer's mess. Yes this man's war is over.

His thoughts were interrupted by a loud knock on his office door. "Enter," he barked.

The young private entered the room. "Sergeant," he said, "we've got a serious situation." "What do you mean 'a serious situation'?" screamed Rock. Jesus, he hated serious situations. He felt his stomach churn.

"Sergeant, that deserter, John Moran, the marine brought in yesterday – he's gone, vanished, gone AWOL, Sergeant."

The blood drained from Rock's face. "What do you mean, 'just vanished'? Jesus Christ, this is a high security compound. Where the fuck's he gone? Christ, don't tell me that a young rookie marine has escaped from a high security compound. Jesus H. Christ, there will be hell to pay. Jesus, heads will roll over this one." His own words brought it home to him with a bang. *His* head would roll. It was the fourth prisoner to escape from his compound in the past few weeks. The brass were out to get him – dishonourable discharge, severance pay cut. Holy sweet Jesus, after twenty-five years of ducking and diving, being shot at and bombed, his career ruined by a greenhorn rookie marine deserter. He slumped back in his chair. Jesus, tomorrow at dawn the marines are coming to pick up the deserter to transport him to the front. What the fuck was he going to do? His mind raced. Yeh sweep the area and leave no stone unturned. Get the bastard no matter what it took.

Jesus, he thought, *after all these years of fucking shit it has to end like this, just when I'm almost home and dry.*

"Private," Sergeant Rock said, "the South Vietnamese were on guard duty last night, weren't they? He probably bribed the guards. You know them slanty eyes are all the same; can't trust the bastards. He's probably out of the Saigon by now and well on his way to Cambodia and there's no way we'll ever see him again." Rock was sure of this. He knew that the South Vietnamese soldiers could not be trusted. A couple of months ago, a couple of North Vietnamese prisoners escaped by bribing the South Vietnamese guards. This bastard had probably gone the same way. But this was different, a very different story; this was no gook; this was a God-damned marine. Those bastard's never gave up. Once you joined the marines you joined for life. This was an entirely different situation. Nobody deserted from the marines. Rock knew they were coming for their man and the marines wouldn't take no for an answer.

Jesus he was in deep shit. What he was going to do? He knew he couldn't talk his way out of this one. His stomach hurt and his head throbbed. He began to shake, this was it: the end of the road for Master Sergeant Rock.

Suddenly the telephone rang interrupting his worried thoughts, a calm voice spoke, an educated voice. Rock knew immediately that it was an officer. "Master Sergeant Rock, you're the port dispatcher aren't you? I've been reliably informed that you're the person I need to speak to."

The calm soft voice had a soothing affect on Rock, he felt his body relax; he slouched back in his chair.

"Now listen sergeant and listen good; this is Captain Grant Master of the USS Neptune just dropped anchor this morning in Saigon docks."

Rock was right; it *was* an officer.

"I've got a situation here sergeant," continued the soft voice, "and I need your help, do I make myself clear?"

Jesus you have a situation! Thought Rock.

The soft voice continued, "It's like this sergeant; I've got a stowaway, a civilian, on my ship. I need to hand him over to you and I want you to get him out of the country quietly. No paperwork, no red tape, we'll cover your expenses well sergeant." The soft voice continued, "Do you understand sergeant? Just get him safely back to Europe with no fuss, have I made myself clear?"

Sergeant Rock couldn't believe what he was hearing, was this some kind of set up? It had to be. He knew they were out to get him and he wouldn't put it past those officers to play dirty. He was cautious.

"So this person," asked Rock inquisitively. "Who is he captain?"

"A nobody," replied Captain Grant. "No name; no papers; just a civilian stowaway on my ship. I want him out of here like he never existed, get him a false passport. Just no paper trail."

Rock's crafty mind began to work overtime. "Captain," he asked, "can you give me a description of this person?"

"He's seventeen years old sergeant; Irish; name of Eddie Kelly; long-haired, hippie freak boarded my ship in Dublin, a stowaway. I just want him out of here just like he's never been to Vietnam. I've been told that you can help me sergeant. And, as I said, you'll be rewarded very well for your assistance."

Rock had done this type of thing before. Officers would unofficially bring their wives and girlfriends out to Vietnam and Rock would arrange the flights and all the necessary paperwork without any fuss. He'd accumulated quite a tidy sum for his retirement sorting out unofficial business for officers but this time it wasn't the money that interested Rock. He knew he could easily arrange a false passport, transportation and the necessary paperwork for the stowaway, there was nothing unusual about that but Rock was thinking about something totally different.

"Okay captain. Consider it done sir," said Rock. "I'll pick your stowaway up at midnight from the ship and by the way I'll need seven hundred dollars when you hand him over for expenses you understand sir. I'll take it from there no hassle or fuss captain. It will be the last you ever see or hear of your Irish hippie."

"It's a deal sergeant," Captain Grant replied. "Be at the Neptune at midnight sergeant." Captain Grant ordered First Officer Peters to get the cash from the bursar for entertainment expenses.

It's all sorted, he thought, smiling. *Another little problem solved. Yes sir, Captain William Grant could still make Admiral.*

PECKER WOODS

Rock sat back in his chair and felt good he was king of his world. His gut felt better, his hangover had lifted and a smile spread across his face. This would be a masterstroke. Jesus H. Christ what a finale from Uncle Sam's army. He'd been pulling stunts on the army since 1942 but this was a whopper nobody could touch him now. He just couldn't stop laughing to himself as he walked the short distance across the dusty compound to the Sergeant's mess for a few Jack Daniels whiskeys to celebrate. That's why they called him Master Sergeant *Lucky* Rock.

Back on the USS Neptune the sailors had made a collection for Eddie. They all felt joy and relief that he was going home. Eddie Kelly was their Irish hero – the accidental stowaway from Ireland the undertaker's assistant and the guy who didn't screw them up with the captain or First officer Peters. The sailors collected almost a thousand dollars for their Irish friend.

"Here buddy," Jerome said. "Me and the guys have made a little collection for you, here take this money to help buy that fancy gravestone for your poor mum back home in Ireland. Yeah buddy get your brother a decent burial plot, one that's fit for a soldier. That's what your mum deserves. We all love you like a brother Eddie and you've got soul bro. Yeh man you're our Irish soul brother and Eddie I'll always be grateful; you never betrayed me and how can I ever forget that?" "And remember this Eddie" he continued "It's not goodbye it's see yah later brother, some other time, some other place."

Eddie was ecstatic; it had been worth it all, sailing half-way around the world just to get the money to buy his ma the grave and the statue.

Jaysus, he thought, *there must be a God after all and he works in strange and wonderful ways.*

One night during the long voyage from Dublin when Eddie got drunk and very homesick, he had told the sailors all about his grandfather Christy Doyle fighting in the Citizen's Army and how the English had killed him. He told them about the Irish army in Katanga and about the murder of his elder brother Paddy killed by the Balubas and his poor desperate mother, who wanted nothing more in life than to get a big marble statue and a fancy grave at the front of Glasnevin cemetery for her dead son Paddy. Eddie nearly had the sailors in tears when he told them how poor they were and how he often had to eat pig's feet or tripe and cow heel for dinner. The sailors' hadn't got a clue what Eddie was talking about – Irish heroes? English soldiers? Balubas? Pig's feet? Tripe and cow heel? Marble statues?

Christ, thought Jerome, *what planet is this guy from? Imagine a guy so poor he has to eat pig's feet and tripe (whatever that was), and we thought that us poor niggers in the States had a rough time. No sir, we know nothing about real poverty like the poor Irish.*

But they loved Eddie and his funny accent and his undertaker's jokes. They understood Eddie's sadness for his dead brother and his mum's grief for her dead son and her wanting the fancy grave and the big marble statue. All the sailor's understood the sadness and poverty of the Kelly family and most of all they all loved poor simple Eddie Kelly who, in a funny way, was just like them – only Irish. Their Irish hero!

Just after midnight, as the full moon lit up the Saigon docks, First Officer Peters of the USS Neptune walked down the gang plank and handed over the roll of bills and the accidental Irish stowaway to Master Sergeant Freddie Rock, dispatcher for the port of Saigon. "He's all yours sergeant," Peters said. "Now you take good care of Mister Kelly and get him home safely."

"Not a problem, sir," replied Master Sergeant Rock. "I sure will take good care of young Mister Kelly. In fact, I have great plans in store for Mister Eddie Kelly." Rock smiled as he looked at his charge. *Good,* he thought. *He fits the bill nicely. I'm sure Mister Kelly will make a first class marine.*

Eddie and Rock walked a short distance without speaking and boarded a waiting army jeep. After an hour's journey from the docks they drove through the streets of Saigon to the military compound. Eddie was amazed at the sights and sounds of the narrow streets of the crowded exotic city; he'd never experienced anything like this before. It reminded him a bit of the fish and fruit market in Moore Street in Dublin, only bigger and brighter, and with all the strange and wonderful smells.

It was the happiest day of his life, his ordeal was over at last and he was going home. Back to his ma and Shaky and his beloved Dublin with the money to help buy his ma her fancy grave and marble statue. He was sure Shaky Shanahan would keep his job for him.

After they drove into the military compound Eddie was taken from the jeep and led into the barrack room and on into Sergeant Rock's office.

Rock sat at his desk and stared hard at Eddie. "Well, well," he said. "What have we got here? A God-damned Irish hippie stowaway. Welcome son, welcome to Vietnam, welcome to Uncle Sam's Army."

His words were followed by hard blows to Eddie's head which knocked him to the barrack room floor blood streaming from his face.

Sergeant Rock looked on without emotion; he'd seen it all before.

Two of the South Vietnamese guards grabbed Eddie roughly and held him upright before Sergeant Rock's desk.

Rock stood up and coldly said, "Listen, son, and listen well, from now on you forget about Eddie Kelly , Dublin and the ship; that's all in the past do you hear me now son? From now on you are Private John Moran, United States Marine Corps, identity number 143840. Forget about your past son from now on you're a marine private first class. You are part of Uncle Sam's army in Vietnam, here to fight those slanty eyed yellow commi bastards who are trying to take over the free world and deprive us of our freedom. Do you hear me now son?"

Rock was on a roll. "Look at it this way; you could say you are representing the Irish people in Vietnam – Ireland's only contribution to the free world's fight against communism."

Eddie's eyes began to swell and blood ran down his nose; he was in a daze. He couldn't understand what was happening. He was supposed to be going home to Ireland, what was all this about? Who the hell was John Moran?

A South Vietnamese soldier held Eddie down as an army barber roughly cut his long hair and shaved his head until nothing was left of his pride and joy, just a crew-cut tight to the skull. Rock searched his pockets and found the roll of money the sailor's had given Eddie, he quickly counted the dollar bills.

"Okay Private Moran," he shouted as he stuffed the roll of dollar bills in his pocket, "that just about covers your haircut and your new clothes you God-damned hippy freak," Rock screamed at Eddie, "Listen son, if I ever hear you mention that ship again or your fucking home in Ireland I'll have you shot. This is your home now son – Uncle Sam's Army. Got the message, Private First Class Moran, Private John Moran serial number 143840, got the message now son?"

Eddie was roughly dressed in green army fatigues and a metal dog tag was hung around his neck and the South Vietnamese guards dragged him from the barrack room to a small dirty cell. He was thrown on a filthy mattress which was lying in the corner of the room.

His body hurt all over, his face was bloody and he just couldn't believe what was happening; it was all a bad dream, a horrible nightmare. He looked at the name on the metal dog tags around his neck. The name read 'John Moran, ID no. 143840, US Marine corps, Private First Class. Christ he wasn't dreaming at all; this was real; this was happening. Jaysus talk about bad luck; he was an undertaker's assistant from Dublin who goes out for a quiet drink on a Friday night and ends up in the United States Marine Corp in a fucking war in some God-forsaken place called Vietnam in the middle of God knows where. Eddie lay down on the dirty mattress and closed his eyes.

He was back in the Ace of Spades, it was a Friday night. He was sitting on his favourite bar stool sipping a cool, creamy pint of Guinness and Terry was behind the bar singing 'Molly Malone' to himself and busy pulling pints for all his thirsty customers. Eddie looked in the mirror and was shocked by his own reflection. His long hair was gone; he was dressed in a green United States Marine uniform. He saw a black face in the mirror. Someone grabbed him and he turned around quickly. Suddenly he woke up with a black military policeman shaking him roughly on the shoulder.

"Private Moran," the military policeman shouted at Eddie. "Stand to, soldier. Orders to move out. On the double, on the double!"

Eddie dragged himself up painfully and was led outside to a waiting truck full of young sleepy faced marines who had just arrived in Saigon.

Eddie was hauled aboard the truck and sat beside a young pimply-faced soldier who looked curiously at Eddie but didn't speak.

Suddenly a voice called, "Private Moran."

Eddie turned to see Sergeant Rock standing at the barrack room door.

Rock shouted, "Private Moran, you have a good war. Grease the slanty eyed little fuckers, grease the little yellow bastards, do you hear me now son? Welcome to Vietnam. Welcome to Uncle Sam's war." Rock laughed loudly as he turned and walked back into the barrack room.

The army truck lurched forward and headed off slowly on a two-hour drive to the Marine Corp forward base at Bein Ley, some forty-five miles north of Saigon. Eddie was tired and hungry when they reached the marine base. He hadn't eaten since he had left the ship and his body ached from the brutal treatment he had received at the hands of the South Vietnamese guards. He thought it strange how none of the soldiers spoke during their long drive from Saigon. They sat heads down, silent, deep in their own thoughts.

As soon as the truck stopped a young officer screamed at the men to dismount and form a straight line. The officer divided the twenty or so men into four groups and pointed to the sand bagged bunkers that were to be their home for their twelve-month tour of duty. As Eddie turned to follow the group of men as they walked towards their allocated bunker the young officer screamed, "Private John Moran, the captain wants to see you on the double, this way Pecker Woods."

The young officer led Eddie into a fortified bunker where a marine captain sat at his desk studying a green-coloured file marked 'John Moran'.

When he saw Eddie he jumped up quickly and screamed, "Moran you are a God-damned deserter, there are no deserters in the United States Marines Corps. Do you hear me, Private Moran? There are no deserters in the Marine Corps. God damn it Moran if the men hear you're a deserter you are a dead man. Do you hear me Private Moran? Next time you're out on patrol you could get a bullet in the back; nobody likes a deserter, especially in the Marine Corp. If you can't trust your buddies out here you're dead. You're better off without them. So listen, Moran; nobody's got to know you're a deserter. Do you hear me, Private Moran? Nobody is to know. I don't want any trouble with my company."

Eddie stood silently listening to the captain speak and as soon as the captain stopped he burst out crying. "Sir, I shouldn't be here at all. Me name's not John Moran, me real name is Eddie Kelly, I'm an undertaker's assistant from Dublin, Ireland, I'm not really a soldier at all sir. I was stranded by accident on a warship from Dublin – the Neptune. I shouldn't be here, it's all a big mistake, I'm an accidental stowaway from Dublin sir. I'm tellin yeh the God's honest truth. Here's the story captain." Eddie rambled on, "It was me Friday night out in Dublin, yeh know the way Friday night is me big night out, captain. After I finished washing and dressing the one legged docker, him who lost his leg in the Great Lock Out with Jim Larkin, him with the seven kids – Hop Along Cassidy they called him, sir. Do yeh get it, sir? Hop Along Cassidy." Eddie laughed nervously. "I went down to me favourite pub – yeh know the one, sir: the Ace of Spades on the quays beside the Liffey– for a few pints like I does every Friday night, before I go to the Go-Go club to meet me girlfriend, Colette Murphy. She's from Sheriff Street and she works in Woolworths in Henry Street, sir. Anyway, I meets a black sailor in the pub – as black as your boot sir – and we got talking- so I invited him around to the Go-Go club to meet me pal but that big bollix, Frankie Coyle the bouncer, wouldn't let me into the Go-Go with the black sailor. Frankie said sailors were too violent and dat's how I ended up back on the big ship that was docked down beside the North Wall: the warship with all the lights. He invited me back to the ship for a drink. I got drunk and the ship left Dublin with me onboard, it was all an accident, sir. I shouldn't be here at all; it's all a big mistake. I was supposed to be sent back to Dublin when the ship reached Vietnam. The captain of the ship told me I was going home, sir, I just don't know what I'm doing here captain. I have to get home to me ma and me job with Shaky Shanahan in the undertakers in Finlater's Place so I do. It's me ma; I'm really worried her about captain, she's not at all well, so she isn't, not since me brother Paddy, was eaten by the Balubas out in Africa when he was in the Irish Army. He was a private in the Padraig Pearse Battalion of the Eastern Command so he was. When they handed me over to Sergeant Rock at the docks he beat me up and robbed all me bleedin money so he did, the money the sailor's gave for the fancy grave and the marble statue for me brother, the one I was telling yeh about sir: me brother who was eaten by the Balubas over in Africa."

The captain stared at Eddie in total disbelief. What in God's name was this guy rambling on about? Christ of all the bullshit stories he'd ever heard in his career this one took the biscuit. An undertaker's assistant-Jesus.

"Listen Moran, what a load of horse crap. Your dog tag says you're Private John Moran and your papers say you're Private John Moran and I say your Private John Moran so shut up with all this bullshit and report to your unit." The captain turned to the young officer. "Take Private Moran over to the quartermaster and get him rigged out in full battle kit, he's out on patrol first thing in the morning in the northern sector"

As he followed the young officer across the dusty compound to the quartermaster's store the captain stood at the bunker door looking at Eddie. He started to laugh. *Christ,* he thought, *is that guy for real? Wait until I tell this one to the guys in the mess tonight. Holy smoke, an undertaker's assistant from Dublin, his brother eaten by Balubas (whoever* they *are), a stowaway on a ship. Jesus did you ever hear such a bullshit story in all your life? Christ, this guy must be some cowardly bastard coming up with a crazy story like that. No,* he thought, *Moran's not going to last long in the jungle. I give him a couple of days at the most and he'll be going stateside in a body bag.*

COWBOYS AND INDIANS

The quartermaster rigged Eddie out in full combat gear from an Aladdin's cave full of the goods and equipment of war. But Eddie was really shocked when he was handed a shiny new black M16 rifle with six clips of ammunition. He had never held a weapon before; he stood there in amazement. It felt like Christmas day when he got a cowboy outfit and a cap firing toy gun.

When he was fully laden with military equipment the young officer led him, struggling under the heavy load, across the compound to a large underground bunker. The officer pointed to a bunk bed near the entrance.

"Moran, that's your cot."

Eddie threw his heavy gear on the floor and sat quietly on the bunk. The bunker was a home to about twelve soldiers – some black, some white. Eddie noticed that all of the white soldiers were sitting on their bunks reading or writing letters. Four or five black soldiers were at the end of the bunker chatting, smoking and drinking, playing the soul music that he had heard on the ship, Tamla Motown, the sailors had called it.

All eyes turned to Eddie. The black soldiers went quiet and started laughing and whispering among themselves.

After a few minutes a young smiling black soldier walked up the bunker to Eddie. "What's going down my man? Welcome to Alpha Company, welcome to our hooch," he said cheerfully to Eddie, holding out his hand.

"I'm cool, man," Eddie replied without even thinking. "Give me five" and he held out his hand. On the long voyage from Dublin, Eddie had picked up the language and moves of the black brothers. It came to him naturally without him even realising it. It was a working class thing.

The black soldier was amazed. "Hell buddy," he said surprised. "You speak the talk of the brothers. Where you are you from, man? Alabama?"

"No, Finglas West," replied Eddie.

"Never heard of that place," said the black soldier looking puzzled. "Is that near Memphis Tennessee?" "No" replied Eddie "it's in Dublin, Ireland". "God-damn brother, you're a long way from home, we all figured you to be a Southern redneck Johnny Reb: white trailer trash from Alabama or some other nigger-hating God-forsaken dump. You have that sort of look about you. Well lord strike me dead," he said smiling. "A white brother! God-damn! Come on, bro," he said, grabbing Eddie's arm. "Come on down and meet the rest of the guys."

Eddie adopted a cool swagger as he walked down to the end of the bunker and was introduced to the rest of the black soldiers. They were surprised at the way Eddie talked their talk and walked their walk. He was immediately accepted. But Eddie also noticed how some of the white soldier's looked at him with coolness and slight hostility in their eyes.

After a few beers, which were Colt 45, he felt very relaxed, just like on the ship with Jerome and Sonny. He felt at ease with the black soldiers for some reason; he was just like them, except he was an undertaker's assistant and they were simply soldiers.

Someone passed Eddie a reefer of marijuana. He had heard about it – weed or grass or whatever they called it. Jerome and Sonny talked a lot about it on the ship, but he had never actually smoked it. He'd looked forward to this moment for a long time– getting high – something different from getting drunk.

He took a deep pull of the joint and felt nothing. He pulled harder on the reefer and the strange tasting smoke caught his breath. Jaysus it was stronger than the Sweet Afton cigarettes that his father smoked. He began to cough loudly much to the amusement of the black soldiers. Suddenly it hit him like a ton of bricks, he felt lightheaded and the room began to spin around him.

"Brothers," he said, "I feel a little sick, I've got to lie down for a while, I'm feeling kind of funny so I am." The smoke on an empty stomach had hit Eddie very hard.

All the black soldiers laughed. "Okay bro, you lie down on your cot and chill out man, take it easy now bro." Eddie just about made it back to his bunk without passing out. He hauled his sore body up on the bed and lay on his back and closed his eyes to stop the room spinning around as the sweet soul music ebbed in and out of his head. After a while the feeling of sickness passed and he began to feel good – very relaxed, very mellow. He was stoned out of his head and he liked the mellow feeling.

When the bad feeling had passed completely he turned on his side and tried to focus on the rest of the soldiers. He noticed that there was a sort of a misty haze around each person in the bunker. The white soldiers had a red angry haze around their bodies which was strongest around their heads. He looked over at the black soldiers who were laughing and joking; they had a sort of purple-coloured haze like a mist around their bodies. *Two tribes*, he thought – *the purple and the red.*

He held up his arm and he noticed that he had a green haze around his hand and his arm. Suddenly it dawned on him; he understood it all; it was so clear, everything made sense. He was Irish and he was from the green tribe – the Irish tribe. Of course, that's why they called it the Emerald Isle.

What if another Irish person walked into the bunker? Yes, they would have a green haze just like him. We're all tribes. Only the green tribe was closer to the black tribe than the red tribe – the white Americans.

What if a protestant walked in like Shaky Shanahan's undertaker friend Harry Flower the freemason? What colour of haze would Harry have? Orange, he thought, laughing to himself. *No, that was wrong – green. We're all Irish, aren't we? Yes,* impressed by his clever deductions, *only they don't know it, yet – a lost tribe,* he thought. *Yes, the orange tribe. The lost tribe of Israel.* His mood changed and he began to feel differently; he began to feel paranoid, very alone. He looked around at the soldiers in the room. They looked distant, almost unreal, like fleeting dark shadows enveloped in a purple or red haze. He realised that he shouldn't be there. This was their space and their time. This was their war not his. He wasn't part of this. This wasn't part of his destiny. It was like he was watching a war film at the cinema and the soldiers in the bunker were all actors. But he wasn't an actor in their war. He was Eddie Kelly, undertaker's assistant from Dublin, employee of Shaky Shanahan, son of Bridie Kelly, brother of dead Paddy Kelly. No, this wasn't his time or place. He began to panic.

What the fuck am I doing here? was his final thought before he passed out? Then he drifted into a beautiful, peaceful dream about Dublin: the smell of the river Liffey; the taste of a pint of Guinness; the crack in the Ace of Spades pub and the jokes with the old men. When he was there he thought it was all boring, but now he realised that he was the boring one, not the old men or the place. He was the problem, not them. He missed the jokes, the Dublin accent, the constant talking, the stories, the world where he belonged. He wanted so much to be back there. Then he dreamt again about that beautiful girl, the dream he'd had back home. It seemed so long ago. He was there again in some strange, faraway place – the jungle with the beautiful girl beside him. But this time it was different, slightly different, than the dreams he'd had before. He wanted to ask her who she was, what her name was. He was just about to reach out his hand to touch her naked body when he was rudely awoken by a loud voice. "Move your God-dammed ass marines, six bells, on the double, on the double. Get out of those God-damn cots, move it soldiers, move it now"

Eddie opened his eyes. He was back in reality with a bang – the horrible reality that he was a marine; he was in Vietnam; he was in Uncles Sam's army fighting in his war. His head felt fuzzy and he found it hard to focus. He looked at the dog tags which read 'John Moran'. He was John Moran marine first class once more.

In a daze he followed the rest of the marines across the compound to the mess tent where he had a couple of cups of strong coffee and smoked a Lucky Strike cigarette that one of the brother's gave him. He had never tasted coffee before his time on the ship and he come to like the strong pungent taste, he began to feel better but not much better.

The mess door opened and the captain and the young officer entered.

"Marines," the officer shouted, "full battle dress; assemble at the heli pad in thirty minutes, you're out on patrol in the northern sector. On the double, on the double."

The soldiers, rushing back to the bunker to ready themselves for their first patrol, quickly emptied the mess. Eddie hadn't got a clue what he was supposed to do so he followed the rest of the men sheepishly and copied their movements as best he could. He dressed in his uniform, put on the new shiny black boots, picked up his rifle, ammunition and hardhat, and followed the rest of the men to the waiting Huey helicopter on the helipad; engines roaring and swirling blades turning slowly and blowing up dust in the morning heat.

He fell in line with the rest of the soldiers, clambered onboard the noisy machine, and sat down on the seat beside the window. His stomach lurched. He'd never been on an aeroplane before let alone a helicopter, he felt like he was in one of the war films he'd seen in the Casino Cinema on a Saturday afternoon; like he was an actor only this was real – a real war.

When all the soldiers were onboard the heavy machine lifted slowly off the ground. The noise of the helicopter engines was deafening and his whole body shook with the vibrations of the noisy machine. His stomach began to churn; his heart beat wildly and sweat poured down his body, he was terrified, so desperate, so hopelessly lost. He gasped for breath; a sense of panic overtook him. He could hardly breathe and was covered in sweat. He closed his eyes tightly; he was afraid to look out the window at the ground below, he thought he was going to faint; his heart raced so fast.

After what seemed like an eternity he could feel the pulsating engines of the helicopter slow down as it hovered over the ground. Eddie felt better; he opened his eyes and through the window could see the ground gently approaching. He looked at the rest of the soldiers and noticed the fear in their eyes but Eddie didn't feel afraid any more just relieved as the helicopter gently touched down in the jungle clearing.

The men began to dismount from the helicopter and run towards the cover of the jungle canapé. Eddie hadn't a clue what he was doing or where he was going so he just fell in behind the soldiers copying their every move.

When they reached the cover of the jungle and found the trail to the village the young officer turned to Eddie and shouted, "Hey Moran you're on point duty move it soldier."

Eddie looked blankly at the officer; he hadn't a clue what point duty meant.

"Move it Pecker Woods, move it!" ordered the young officer.

"Sir," Eddie said, "I don't know what point duty is sir."

The young officer's face went red and he screamed at Eddie. "God-damn Moran, what kind of a soldier are you? You're on a charge, Moran – disobeying orders – and when we get back to base I'm reporting you to the captain." As he looked at Eddie he wondered what kind of soldier this was. There was something not quite right about Private John Moran, he didn't walk like a soldier or look like a soldier. Yeh there was something very odd about this guy, something very odd indeed. Private Moran needs some serious sorting out. Even the greenest rookie after six weeks in Paris Island, after basic training, had the look of a soldier; this guy is a goddamned impostor. Then he remembered what the captain had told them in the officer's mess regarding Moran's cock and bull story about not being a marine and the bullshit about being an undertaker's assistant from Ireland. He laughed. *No way,* he thought. *This guy's a God-damned liar and a coward to boot. Christ, an undertaker's assistant. Holy Jesus he's in the right place for an undertaker. Jesus, what a bullshit story.*

"Listen, Moran; forget about point duty. Just follow the rest of the patrol and as soon as we get back to base I'm reporting you to the captain."

Eddie saw the look of bewilderment in the young officer's eyes. He wondered if the penny had finally dropped: if the young officer knew he wasn't a real soldier and believed him. When they got back to the base the young officer would explain everything to the captain then they would realise he was telling the truth and, finally, he would be sent home.

Magic Words

From their landing zone Alpha Company headed into the jungle and in single file followed the trail towards the village. The companies' orders were to march from the landing zone and carry out a search operation in the surrounding area to try and locate the North Vietnamese regulars who came at night to steal food and terrorise the villagers. The American's were trying to persuade the villagers to leave their homes and move closer to Saigon into a secure zone safe from the Vietcong.

The march to the village was over three kilometres and in the sweltering jungle heat and Eddie found the going very tough. He could hardly move with his heavy equipment and his feet began to swell and blister against the new leather of his heavy army boots, he was causing problems for the company, holding them back. They had to reach the village and carry out their search before nightfall to allow the Huey helicopter to return and pick them up safely in the clearing on the edge of the jungle. Any delay was highly dangerous. The helicopters could not operate safely in the dark and if they missed their airlift Alpha Company were stranded in the jungle, which was a very deadly place at night for American soldiers. The night belonged to the North Vietnamese and the day belonged to the Americans.

Eddie was hurting bad, he could barely move his body, his feet were bleeding and his military gear felt like a ton weight on his back. He began to fall behind the rest of the company and the young officer was getting increasingly impatient with him.

"For Christ's sake Moran," he called, "get a move on you fucking asshole you're compromising the whole company."

The young officer finally lost his patience. "Fuck you Moran, God-damn you now soldier you're on your own buddy". The soldier's marched on quickly towards the village leaving Eddie limping along and getting further behind the company with each step he took. Finally Eddie was finished. He just gave up; he just couldn't go any further he just wanted to lie down and die; he didn't care anymore what happened, he'd reached the end; he just couldn't walk any further. Finally he lay down on the jungle path his body covered in sweat, his feet swollen and his whole body aching from head to toe. With great difficulty he just about managed to pull off his boots to ease his crippled feet. He took a gulp of water from his canteen and rested his head on his haversack and drifted into a deep slumber, he was totally exhausted.

It was the loud screeching of bird's that woke him up abruptly from his deep sleep and then, a split second later, a massive explosion rocked the jungle. Eddie knew there had been some kind of explosion – a bomb or something – but he wasn't sure what to do.

Without thinking he jumped up quickly leaving all his equipment (including his rifle) behind and in his bare feet he limped up the jungle trail towards the noise. After a couple of hundred yards he could smell it – that acrid smell of smoke and burning flesh. When he turned the bend in the trail on the outskirts of the village he suddenly stopped, horrified at what he saw. It was like a scene out of hell. Eddie was used to dead bodies; he had seen mutilated bodies after car crashes and accidents, burnt bodies, all sorts of bodies and it didn't bother him, but this was something totally different. Arms, legs and pieces of blood-smeared cloth hung from the trees. But it was the bird's that scared Eddie most of all. Alpha Company had walked into a Vietcong ambush.

A huge bomb had been planted on the trail just outside the village which was detonated by the Vietcong as the American soldiers passed by killing and mortally wounding everyone in the patrol.

There was hundreds of screeching bird's flapping wildly in the air. They seemed to be trying to pick at, and eat, the bits of burnt flesh hanging from the trees.

As the smoke began to clear he could see the crumpled bodies of the mutilated soldier's lying on the ground. Men were crying out. They all seemed to be calling for their mothers. "Mother" or "Mummy", "Help me! Help me!"

Eddie stood there unable to move frozen on the spot. Suddenly, black-clad figures appeared some distance up the trail, carrying rifles.

Christ, it must be the Vietcong, Eddie thought. Then he heard the sound of automatic gunfire. Bullets whizzed through the trees around him and sounded like bumble bees flying by so close he could feel the hot air against his skin.

Suddenly, he felt as if a sledgehammer had hit him on the leg then an explosion of pain. He looked down in slow motion and saw blood running down his leg, a bullet had grazed his thigh. He instinctively put his hand on the wound to try and stop the blood which was pumping out of the gaping gash before he collapsed, face down on the ground.

Darkness began to fall. Eddie wasn't sure if it was nightfall or if he was he dying. He'd often wondered what it was like to die: everything in slow motion, the light fading, everything getting darker. He reached up and ripped off his dog tags with his bloody hands and flung them away; if he was going to die he didn't want to die as John Moran, an American marine.

He could hear the Vietcong as they moved closer, laughing and joking, talking in a strange language. They stopped over each wounded American soldier and fired a single shot into the head making sure they were dead. As they approached, the screams of the American soldiers got louder and louder; they knew they were going to die and their dying words were, "Mother, Mother," until the single shot silenced them.

He could hear them getting closer to him by the second, he tried to move but his body was anchored to the ground. By now the Vietcong soldiers were only a few feet away. It was their laughing that scared him most of all; they seemed to enjoy murdering the injured soldiers as they lay dying and screaming for their mothers.

Eddie began to shiver, his body felt cold, he was scared. He closed his eyes and waited for the single shot which he knew was only a few seconds away. Would Paddy be waiting for him in Heaven? What would Paddy think when he saw him in his American marine uniform? Thinking of Paddy brought a sad smile to his face. He remembered the time he lay on the ground in the schoolyard of Finglas Primary School all those years ago, battered and bruised, when Paddy had picked him. He remembered Paddy's words:

"Little fella if you're ever frightened or ever need me just say the magic words – Paddy, Paddy – and I'll be there to help yeh."

By now the Vietcong soldiers were almost upon him and he could clearly hear their laughing and joking and the cries of the dying soldiers. "Mother, Mother. Help me. Help me."

He opened his tear filled eyes and softly called out the magic words: *"Paddy, Paddy. Help me, for Jaysus sake help me Paddy! Help me! Help me!"* As Eddie slipped into unconsciousness he was aware of someone lifting him off the ground and he felt himself being dragged along the jungle floor and the shouting and the laughter of the Vietcong soldiers began to fade slowly into the distance until he could hear it no more.

He tried to look up, but he couldn't; he was too weak. That was Eddie's last thought as everything went black. He was unconscious for almost three days.

It was a small dark room, dimly lit by the pale moonlight shining through a window opening. Eddie was confused. At first, he thought he was home, lying in bed in his small Corporation bedroom in Finglas, having his beautiful dream. His leg hurt. Then he realised he was lying on a straw mattress in the corner of a small room; it felt strange but vaguely familiar. His mind began to focus. He realised he was naked, his leg bound tightly in a form of bandage. Then he became aware that there was somebody in the room standing close to him. He focused hard in the semi-darkness on the small figure standing by his side. It was her – the same beautiful girl he dreamt about. A tingle of excitement ran through his body. He reached out his hand to touch her. As his hand got closer to her body he expected his father to shout, "Get out of that bed yeh lazy bastard" and his beautiful dream would be over but no, this time he could touch her and he feel the warmth of her soft dark skin. The young girl gave Eddie a bowl of rice and some water and he tried to talk to her but the young girl did not understand his words. He gulped down the food; he was starving. After he had eaten he tried to get up but his legs felt like jelly and he collapsed back on the bed drifting in and out of unconsciousness for several days. Every night without fail the young girl would come with food and water for Eddie and dress his wounded leg.

After a week or so he began to feel better, stronger, and with some discomfort was able to get off the bed and limp painfully around the room. One evening he hobbled to the door of the hut and realised that he was in a small deserted village with no signs of life. As he stood at the doorway the young girl came screaming up the path shouting angrily at Eddie. He could not understand what she was saying but he knew she wanted him back inside. There was a look of deep fear in her eyes as she pointed at the jungle shouting "Vietcong! Vietcong!" Eddie knew exactly what she meant.

As the days passed slowly Eddie got stronger and more restless by the day. He felt alone and isolated and with a constant fear of capture by the Vietcong soldiers. He began to feel more and more depressed; he just wanted an end to his horrible never ending nightmare.

He couldn't stop thinking about the American soldiers who had been killed in the ambush although he hardly even knew them; he couldn't even remember one of their names. But what about their mothers? The soldiers were dead but their poor mothers, wife's and families were left to suffer, left with all the grief.

Christ, he thought, smiling, *I'm beginning to sound like ould Shaky Shanahan so I am*

He wondered why the American Army hadn't searched for him and most importantly who had rescued him from the Vietcong soldiers, saved his life and brought him to the village?

He vaguely remembered being pulled through the jungle away from the Vietcong soldiers but most of all he remembered the screams of the dying American marines and how they all called for their mothers before they died.

When Eddie thought he was going to die he didn't call for his mother but for his dead brother Paddy. Had Paddy come and saved his life? Had the magic word's worked? He didn't know but he did know that he was alive and someone had dragged him away from certain death at the hands of the Vietcong soldiers.

The night before Eddie's patrol had landed in the jungle clearing; the Vietcong had raided the village and took all the young men away to join the Vietcong army to fight the Americans. The young girl and her father, who was the village elder, had a lucky escape and hid from the Vietcong in the jungle. Her father knew that if they caught him he would be shot immediately because of his support for the Americans, he was also afraid of his daughter being raped and killed. He had pleaded with the villagers to leave and move to the American safe zone but his people were reluctant to leave their homes and farms but it was too late now.

The young girl and her father hid, waiting for the American patrol to arrive, as they did most days. They were relieved when they heard the noise of the helicopter early the next morning. They were safe; the soldiers would save them and take them far away from the clutches of their enemy.

They left their hiding place and followed the American soldiers up the trail towards the village. Suddenly they heard a massive explosion that shook the earth and echoed through the jungle, they knew it was a Vietcong ambush.

At first the young girl's father wanted to run and hide but he decided to follow the trail and see what happened to the Americans; they were still their best chance of escape. Then they reached the scene of carnage. They found the jungle trail littered with the dead and mutilated bodies of the American soldiers. A short distance away they stumbled upon a young soldier with a bullet wound in his leg lying on the ground and crying like a baby. Then they saw the Vietcong soldiers approaching.

The young girl knelt down beside the young soldier who kept shouting out words she couldn't understand, he looked so helpless lying there; he was so young and frightened. She beckoned to her father to help the wounded soldier and with some effort they dragged him off the trail into the cover of the jungle and away from danger. When darkness fell they carried the unconscious soldier to their hut in the now-deserted village. They knew it wasn't safe in the village but they had no choice, they had to shelter the wounded soldier somewhere.

The young girl's father decided to try and contact the Americans; he knew they would come searching for the patrol the following day. He set off at night leaving his daughter to look after the wounded soldier. A short distance from the village he was spotted by a patrol of Vietcong regulars and didn't stand a chance – he died instantly in a hail of AK47 bullets.

In the deserted village the young girl undressed Eddie and cleaned his wound. The wound wasn't serious: just a deep graze above the knee like a long burn mark.

She studied him closely as he lay sleeping. He was very young with a kind face; he didn't look like a soldier to her, at least not like the rest of the Americans; he looked so young and so innocent. As she gazed at the young man lying on the mattress she wondered who he was, what his name was, where he was from, was he married? Then she thought about his family, his poor mother all those thousands of miles away in America worried about her young son. Then she noticed it, the tattoo on the young mans arm. It looked very strange to her. An unfamiliar symbol and some very strange words which she didn't understand.

He looked so beautiful and so peaceful lying there, his slim body reflected in the pale moonlight, his long soft hands and his kind face, too kind for a soldier's face and his skin. As she ran fingers down his arm she was struck by the softness of his skin, so soft, so tender. She would protect him and make him better for his mother's sake. Yes, she would make her soldier well and save him from the Vietcong soldiers and get him back safely to the Americans, back to his home and his family in the United States.

Love's Old Sweet Song

Master Sergeant 'Lucky' Rock sat alone in the sergeant's mess looking out over the dusty compound and the neat line of shiny green army trucks. His gut hurt; he'd drunk too much sour mash again last night; he was celebrating. As usual he'd outsmarted the army and dug himself out of a very deep hole. If that Irish hippy freak hadn't turned up on the warship he would have been in very deep shit but as usual he came out of the situation on top and was flying home stateside in a couple of weeks. Sergeant 'Lucky' Rock's war would soon be over.

The young private entered the sergeant's mess and handed Rock a note.

"This better be important," he said to the young private.

"It is sergeant."

Rock read the note and turned to the private. "Dismissed."

The private turned and left the mess.

Rock had the same feeling he got when he'd shot the young German boy soldier all those years ago. First he felt slightly guilty then thought to himself, *fuck him, fuck the God-damned Irish hippy, he would have died of drugs anyway. Nobody's going to miss him. He's a nobody, a fucking low life, a fucking undertaker's assistant.* He laughed nervously.

He ordered himself a large Jack Daniels and finished it in one gulp.

It was the isolation and then the boredom that began to affect Eddie badly; it was like been locked in a cell with no one to talk to, day after day, night after night.

Of all the pain that Eddie had suffered as an accidental stowaway it was the isolation and boredom that affected him most of all. He couldn't go outside the hut and was in constant fear of being captured by the Vietcong. He spent the long days lying on his bed drifting in and out of sleep and thinking of

Dublin city, his family and about when he and Paddy were young. He kept himself sane by vividly imagining the times he spent as a child on Sandymount strand on beautiful summer days all those many long years ago.

During the summer holidays his mother would take her two young sons on day trips to the beach where they would meet Florrie and Greta who would bring jam sandwiches and hot sweet tea in a jam jar. He would lie on the mattress for hours thinking about Sandymount strand. He could smell the sea; he could hear the waves crashing against the shore and the seagull's screeching overhead fighting over crusts of bread that Paddy had thrown them. The gentle wave's lapping at his feet; he and Paddy making sand castles; his ma and Aunties Florrie and Greta laughing and joking. In the background he could hear the sound of the church bell ringing from the Star of the Sea Church just across the road: the church where he was baptised, where his ma and da were married. The church where some day he would marry Colette Murphy if he ever survived his terrible ordeal. Star of the Sea. Star of Love. Star of Hope. He could taste the Hughes Brothers ice cream the Tayto cheese and onion crisps and the sharp sweet taste of the Fanta fizzy orange drink when he was dying of the thirst on those long, hot summer days when he was a child. Then the house in Bath Avenue; he could remember every single feature of that house in the most minute detail.

After a long day on the strand, as evening fell, they would walk the short distance to the gloomy terraced red brick house in Bath Avenue with its funny smells and the two cats. The cats frightened him and Paddy. They would lie on the mat in the living room in front of the fireplace, the good room, silently licking their paws, looking at the boys suspiciously, never losing eye contact – sad memories.

He remembered the room so well. The bay window, the high ornate ceilings and especially the large black marble fireplace which was the focal point of the room. On one side of the mantelpiece was a faded photograph in a tarnished silver frame of his grandfather standing proudly outside of Liberty Hall in his Citizen's Army uniform, a smile on his handsome face, and on the other side a picture of James Connolly. An old faded green coloured flag with silver stars, which once belonged to his grandfather, hung over the fireplace. The Starry Plough – the flag of the Dublin workers, the flag of the Citizen's Army. In the centre of the mantelpiece stood a black marble plaque with gold Celtic lettering which read:

However it may be for others, for us of the Citizen's Army there's but one ideal – an Ireland ruled and owned by Irish men and women, sovereign and independent from the centre to the sea and flying its own Irish flag outwards over all the oceans of the world.

James Connolly, 1915
The Worker's Party

It was always the same: sweet sherry for the ladies and fizzy lemonade and sweet sticky cake for him and Paddy. After a few sherries, his ma, Florrie and Greta would get a bit merry; Florrie would play the out-of-tune piano and Greta, in a croaky voice, would always sing their favourite song, 'Love's Old Sweet Song'.

Even today we hear loves song of yore.
Deep in our hearts it dwells forever more.
Footsteps may falter; weary grow the way.
Still we can hear it, at the close of day.
So till the end, when lives dim shadow fall,
Love will be found, love will be found,
The sweetest song of all.

Eddie and Paddy would hide behind the sofa scared of their two old aunts with their funny smell and the two cats. For years Eddie thought that every child in Dublin had two old spinster aunts who had two cats and lived in a terraced house in Sandymount with a funny smell who sang 'Love's Old Sweet Song' accompanied by an out-of-tune piano. And that's where it all began for his brother Paddy, wanting to be like his grandfather, a soldier of the Irish Republic, a soldier of destiny.

Sometimes Eddie imagined that he was sitting with all his mates around a blazing fire up in the fields behind his house in Finglas laughing at Anto's corny jokes and swigging from a flagon of dry sweet cider. It was night time and in the distance he could clearly see the flickering lights of Dublin city and even count the twinkling star's shining like diamonds in the beautiful clear night sky above. He would search the night sky for the outline of the starry plough like the one on his grandfathers Citizen Army's flag.

He often imagined it was a summer's day when the sky was clear and he could see the Dublin Mountains from the fields beside Saint Patrick's well near the village: the gently sloping mountains in the distance to the south framing the shimmering heat rising from the city warmed by the summer sunshine. He would just make it out, half-way up the gentle slope of the mountain: a tiny black speck, barely visible in the distance – The Hell Fire Club: a notorious club for the rich Anglo Irish gentry of Dublin in the last century where rumours of drunkenness and debauchery abounded. The story was told that one night the devil appeared to the drunken revellers while they were playing cards. Someone dropped a card on the floor and when he bent down to pick it up he saw that one of the men at the table had cloven feet – the sign of the devil. On being discovered, the devil jumped up and disappeared up the chimney in a blinding flash leaving a hoof print on the wall above the fireplace.

This story always held great fascination for Eddie and his pals. They would spend hour after hour scaring themselves silly with talk about the Hell Fire club and the appearance of the devil. Eddie was determined to visit the building one day and see for himself where the devil allegedly appeared and left his mark. He finally got his chance when Shaky Shanahan gave him a week's holiday in August. There were few deaths in Dublin in the month of August for some reason nobody wanted to die in the good weather and things were very quiet for the undertakers in the city. With his holiday pay in his pocket and a week off work Eddie invited Colette Murphy to come with him up to the Dublin Mountains for a daytrip to visit the Hell Fire club. Eddie had a plan: he could kill two birds with the one stone: a bit of romance and a chance of God-knows-what and also an opportunity to see the notorious Hell Fire club that he had always wanted to visit. He met Colette, who had taken a day off work, on a sunny Monday morning in O'Connell Street and they got on an empty bus to Dargan just below the Dublin Mountains. Colette was in fantastic form delighted that Eddie was taking her out on a rare trip, she half expected him to propose to her. Some chance. She was wearing a mini skirt (much to Eddies delight). God he felt so hot.

As she clambered clumsily over fences on their way up the side of the mountain towards the Hellfire club Eddie got an odd glimpse of Colette's white underwear and her beautiful long sexy legs. The sight nearly gave Eddie a heart attack. God how he loved Colette Murphy.

The couple nervously entered the gaunt derelict stone building which, despite the warm sunny day, was cold dark and smelt of rot and decay. It gave them the shivers. For some reason Eddie began to feel strangely excited. He felt the hair's stand up on the back of his neck and a cold sweat run down his back. He put his arms around Colette and kissed her passionately. Suddenly the stillness of the air was shattered by the screeching of birds in the open roof timbers above. Colette panicked and ran out of the building shaking with fear followed by a reluctant Eddie.

They lay in the long grass some distance from the ruined building and looked over the sprawling city below. In the distance they could see Howth Head at the northern tip of Dublin Bay and Dalkey to the south. Eddie could just about see Finglas on the northern outskirts of the city through the shimmering haze rising from the city.

The emotion of fear had a very strong effect on their mutual passion. God they were so excited the two of them, locked together, groping, kissing, fondling.

"Eddie, we can't do it. Stop it now. Stop it now. It's not right. We have to wait till we're married before we can go all the way."

Eddie lost all interest in the Hell Fire club after that day and he never did get to see if indeed the devil left his hoof print on the wall above the fireplace. He never took Colette out on a daytrip again. It just wasn't worth the trouble.

These memories kept Eddie sane. He would lie patiently all day thinking about his childhood and his past life, every minute detail, just to pass the time until the young girl came when darkness fell. She became the focus of his whole life, his only contact with a fellow human being. She looked so delicate and soft, not like Irish girls, not like Colette Murphy. One night when she finished dressing Eddie's wound; he put out his hand and touched her face. He could smell her; he could feel the heat of her body. She responded to Eddie's touch by gently kissing his face. Her soft touch made him cry and tears run down his cheeks. It was the touch of another human that opened his heart, the soft touch of a woman, the woman of his dreams. Nobody had ever touched him so gently or softly before. The young girl put her arms around Eddie to comfort him. He felt his soul opening up and a wave of emotion rush out. Eddie's whole body tingled with sexual excitement; he had never felt this intense sort of excitement before. Sometimes with Colette Murphy, when he got lucky, he had felt sexual excitement when she would touch him through his trousers and arouse him but this was something totally different. Eddie kissed the young girl softly on the lips and she responded by gently embracing him.

Eddie could feel the warmth and energy emanating from her body as they lay on the bed, arms and legs entwined in a passionate embrace. Eddie had never experienced this feeling before; his only experience of sex was kissing and groping in a dark lane on a Friday night with Colette Murphy after six pints of Guinness – crude and brutal, the Irish way! This was something totally different; their bodies and minds seemed to fuse together as if they were one person, one being.

The young girl slipped out of her loose clothing and lay naked on the bed. Eddie embraced her tenderly and slid between her open legs. They kissed passionately and Eddie probed gently. He never thought sex would be like this. This was no drunken fumble on a Friday night, this was the best thing Eddie had ever experienced in his life; it was the closest he had ever felt to another human being.

As they gazed into each other's eyes they understood each other; they were communicating without language, without barriers. Finally their mutual passion exploded as they reached orgasm together. It was sheer ecstasy for Eddie.

At that moment it all became clear to him, the reason why he had the strange dreams at home in Dublin. It was her, his first real love and he had to travel halfway across the world to meet her, to fulfil his dreams. That's what the strange dreams were all about, now he understood everything.

The young lovers lay entwined together in the darkness of the deserted village in total happiness and contentment. Eddie was so happy; he even forgot about Dublin. He was thousands of miles from his home and family, wounded, lucky to have escaped with his life, but it didn't matter one bit; he was happier than he had ever been in his whole life. He felt totally content just lying there with her in his arms and he didn't even know her name.

She had lived in fear for most of her young life forced out of her village and most of her family and friends were either dead or in captivity with the Vietcong. But none of this mattered, nothing really mattered, not while she lay on the mattress with her kind, gentle soldier holding her softly in his arms and the touch of his lovely soft tender skin.

The passion and love of the young couple transcended all things – at least for a while.

Suddenly Eddie felt the young girl's body tense. A look of terror appeared in her eyes, she started to shake with fear. He could feel her heart beating wildly against his chest. She had heard something and it terrified her. Eddie froze and listened; he could hear voices outside the hut. Suddenly several soldiers appeared in the doorway. Terror struck Eddie's heart; he knew it was the Vietcong. Just when things were getting better, another nightmare. He would be killed this time and this time, there was no way out. This was the end; he was sure of it.

The dark menacing figures entered the room and pointed their guns at Eddie and the young girl lying on the bed, holding each other tightly and shaking with fear. The soldiers dragged Eddie, naked, out of the hut, through the village and into the jungle. He heard the young girl screaming and a couple of minutes later a single shot rang out. Eddie knew they had killed her. A feeling of utter desolation rippled through his body. He fell on his knees his hands beating the jungle floor in anger and despair. He began to shiver, his heart raced and he fought to catch his breath. He felt as if his soul had been ripped out. He screamed in hurt and anger."Bastards, fuckin little bastards, dat's what yeh are, little yellow murderin fuckers" He wished they would just kill him and get it over with. Eddie didn't want to live anymore. At that moment, there was nothing left to live for. He had come all the way to Vietnam just to meet her and make his dreams come true. He had met his Vietnamese girl and now she was dead. Although he grieved for Paddy his sense of loss for his Vietnamese lover was inconsolable. He was going to be shot and probably tortured in the dark stinking jungle somewhere far away from his home, his beautiful girl dead; nobody would ever know what happened to Eddie Kelly.

SOLDIERS OF IRELAND

They marched all night along the twisting jungle path without stopping, Eddie was naked; his leg hurt, his feet were bleeding. Every time he stumbled he was hit on the back with a rifle butt. He didn't feel the pain anymore, it just didn't matter, he just wished they would shoot him and put him out of his misery. At day break after a gruelling night's march they finally reached a clearing in the jungle on which stood a group of scattered huts. This was the forward base for the Vietcong regulars operating in the northern sector. Eddie was taken to a small hut for interrogation by a Vietcong intelligence officer. The intelligence officer studied his prisoner closely. No dog tags, minor gunshot wound on thigh. Then he noticed it; the most striking thing of all about his prisoner, the tattoo on his arm. The tattoo fascinated the officer. It was the military insignia of the Irish Defence Forces: a circle with eight pointed stars on the outside, the letters F. F. in the centre and below the words 'Oglaigh na hEireann', meaning 'Soldiers of Ireland'. He grabbed Eddies arm and closely studied the strange script, he immediately thought it was French.

So he addressed Eddie in French. Eddie didn't respond. The officer lit a cigarette and looked hard at the prisoner that stood before him. There was something about the captive that baffled him, he just couldn't quite figure out what it was. He began to question Eddie in broken English repeatedly asking his name. Eddie knew that his Irish army tattoo had intrigued his interrogator; He was aware that the tattoo was important; he had a plan that might just save his life. He replied to the interrogator's questions not in English but in the few words he knew of the Irish language, the few words that he had barely managed to learn from Brother O' Cahill at the Christian Brother School in Glasnevin. It was the first time he had ever spoke Irish outside of the classroom.

He spoke his name and where he was from: "Mise Eamann O' Callaig as Baile Atha Cliath, cupla focal, cupla focal."

He kept repeating the few words of Irish he knew repeatedly over and over again. Eddie was certain that he would be shot immediately if they thought that he was an American soldier.

The interrogator became increasingly frustrated with his prisoner. Finally he snapped. He slapped Eddie hard in the face and Eddie reeled back in shock his face stung and his whole body shook with uncontrollable anger. In a blind rage Eddie, mustering all the strength he could, lunged forward and tried to punch the officer, the officer stepped back avoiding contact. Eddie was more shocked at his sudden action than the stunned intelligence officer who immediately shouted for the guard's who rushed in and repeatedly hit Eddie with their rifle butts ,knocking him unconscious to the ground. Finally they dragged his limp body from the hut and threw him roughly into a small bamboo cage. The intelligence officer was convinced that the prisoner was not an American soldier. The script on the tattoo and the language he spoke weren't English? Finally he came to the conclusion that the prisoner was a soldier from an unidentified country fighting with the Americans in the northern sector and was probably wounded in the ambush some weeks before. They were aware that several countries were providing military support to the United States so it was important for them to determine the nationality of the prisoner.

The intelligence officer was ordered by his superiors in Hanoi to send Eddie to the city for further questioning. He was given army fatigues, which were too small for him, blindfolded his hands tied behind his back and thrown on the back of an ancient truck with two armed guards to start the long journey to Hanoi driving only at night to avoid the constant bombing of the American air force. During the day the truck was camouflaged under heavy jungle foliage to avoid the American bombers.

His Vietcong guards were a father and son and the father had been fighting foreign armies occupying Vietnam all of his life: first the French and now the Americans. His son was the same age as Eddie and when they stopped during the day he would remove the blindfold and untie Eddie's hands to allow him to eat a bowl of cold rice and then relieve himself in the jungle.

He noticed the paleness of Eddie's skin and his long soft hands. He told his father that he was sure that the prisoner was not an American soldier but a doctor.

For almost a week they travelled along the bumpy roads until the accidental Irish stowaway and his father and son Vietcong captors finally reached the North Vietnamese capital of Hanoi.

Several Vietcong intelligence officers, including a Russian agent, questioned Eddie. The Russian was fluent in several languages and addressed Eddie in English, French, German and Italian but Eddie only responded with the few words of the Irish language he knew repeating the same words over and over again.

The Russian agent was puzzled by the words Eddie spoke. He had never heard a language like this before; at first he thought it was Danish or Norwegian, a Norse language. He was also puzzled by the strange script of Eddie's tattoo. He studied carefully the words on Eddie's arm but the words made no sense the words were unknown to him.

Finally the Vietcong lost patience with Eddie and decided to execute their unknown prisoner the following day. Before they did however the Russian agent contacted KGB headquarters in Moscow to report the unknown prisoner. The decision had been made -Eddie Kelly was to be executed and it was only a matter of time.

RUSSIAN SIGNALS

Late at night at C.I.A. headquarters in Saigon an intelligence officer was monitoring radio signals between the Communist forces. Suddenly he picked up a strange signal from a Russian agent in the Vietcong headquarters in Hanoi to K.G.B. headquarters in Moscow. The intelligence officer was puzzled when he decoded the Russian message. The message read:

Wounded soldier captured in jungle by Vietcong regulars. Soldier: white Caucasian. Nationality not identified. Speaks unidentified language. Possibly part of covert foreign army fighting with American forces. Has military tattoo on arm with words 'Oglaigh na hEireann' and the letters F.F. in the centre. Can Professor of Linguistics at Moscow University identify language and confirm nationality of prisoner?

The intelligence officer was confused, what the hell was this all about? He picked up the phone and called the Head of Operations.

"Mister Keating, sir," he said, "We've just picked up a signal between Hanoi and Moscow. The V.C. have captured a wounded soldier in the northern sector but they don't think he's American, they can't understand the language he speaks or establish where he's from; can you come down to the operation's room sir and take a look at the signal?"

Keating carefully studied the message and was puzzled at what he read. What the hell was a wounded non-American soldier doing in the northern sector? He remembered that there was a company of marines wiped out by the Vietcong regulars in an ambush a couple of weeks before. There were no survivor's just bits of bodies and every last dog tag was recovered. Who the hell was this guy? Where the hell was he from? He couldn't be American; *no he's not one of ours* he thought. Then he looked at the signal again. 'Oglaigh na hEireann' – strange words, they just don't make any sense at all.

It was later that night when Keating was brushing his teeth before going to bed that it suddenly dawned on him. It was the word 'Eire, Eire, Eireann'; it was vaguely familiar, he knew he'd seen it somewhere when he was stationed in Dublin some years before. Yes that's where he'd seen the word – the Gaelic name for Ireland.

Jesus Christ, he thought, *Ireland. He's fucking Irish. Jesus H Christ, what's a wounded Irish soldier doing in the jungle? Who the hell is this guy?*

He decided to check with the Embassy in Ireland to confirm that his assumptions were correct and the words were indeed Irish. He called the American Embassy in Dublin and the phone was answered by O'Shea in the operation's room.

"O'Shea! O'Shea! It's Keating in Saigon, you'll never believe this. We've just picked up a signal between Vietcong headquarters in Hanoi and the K.G.B. in Moscow – something about a wounded soldier they captured in the jungle. He's not an American; they can't understand the language he speaks or establish his identity however he has a tattoo on his arm – with the words 'Oglaigh na hEireann' and with F. F. in the centre. That's Irish, isn't it O'Shea?"

O'Shea sat in his chair dumbfounded; he felt a tingle run down his spine.

"Yes I think it's Gaelic for Irish Army or some bullshit like that but this is crazy, what the hell would a wounded Irish soldier be doing in a combat zone in Vietnam?" Then suddenly it dawned on him. No it couldn't be – impossible.

He remembered his meeting in the Flowing Tide with Detective Brannigan who was convinced that the missing Dublin lad was on the warship the Neptune which sailed to Vietnam. No it couldn't be, no way. Even if the lad was on the ship what would he be doing in a combat zone? It just couldn't be the Irish lad; it just didn't make any sense, no sense whatsoever.

Across the city in his dark office Detective Basher Brannigan sat in his chair sipping a Powers whiskey from his tea stained mug and waiting patiently for the first phone call of the night. A suicide, a body fished out of the Liffey; it could be anything. Nothing shocked Basher Brannigan anymore. He'd seen it all.

He often played a little game with himself trying to guess what the first call would be. He would sit in the darkness sipping his whiskey and staring at the phone waiting for the ring that would inevitably come. It always did. When the phone did ring he expected to hear that a dead body had been found floating in the Grand Canal or dragged out of the Liffey but instead he was surprised to hear O'Shea from the American Embassy on the line.

"Brannigan, I've just received a message from Saigon. One of our intelligence officers' picked up a signal from the Vietcong to the Russians, it appears that the Vietcong have captured a wounded soldier, non-American, who speaks an unidentifiable language and you're never going to believe this Brannigan; he has what we think is a Gaelic tattoo on his arm with the words 'Oglaigh na hEireann'. That's Irish isn't it? Listen, Brannigan I know it's a long shot but you know that young lad who went missing, the Kelly guy you spoke to me about, he wouldn't happen to have an 'Oglaigh na hEireann' tattoo on his arm by any chance, would he, I was just wondering?"

Basher Brannigan could not believe what he was hearing. "Christ, O'Shea. Tattoo or no bleedin tattoo; it's Eddie Kelly. It has to be. Do yeh think the bleedin Irish Army has invaded Vietnam or what? He was on that ship that sailed to Vietnam all along wasn't he, the ship that docked in Dublin the night he disappeared? I knew he went to Vietnam, I knew all along that Eddie was on that fuckin ship and you wouldn't listen to me, how the fuck did he end up a prisoner, you did say he was wounded didn't yeh, how the fuck did he get wounded, he's not a fuckin soldier fighting in the war is he? Anyway, where's Eddie now?"

"He's being held by the Vietcong in Hanoi" replied O Shay.

"And where the fuck is Hanoi when it's at home?"

"Vietnam, Brannigan. North Vietnam."

"Tattoo or no bleedin tattoo its Eddie. It has to be. And by the way, O'Shea, Eddie does speak a strange unidentifiable language: it's his bleedin Dublin accent. No wonder the Vietcong can't understand a word he says. He was on that ship wasn't he? The ship that went to Vietnam. Jaysus he goes out for a drink in Dublin on a Friday night and ends up a prisoner in fuckin Vietnam. Jaysus O'Shea it's all your fuckin fault; you just wouldn't listen to me now would you?

"Calm down! Calm down!" said O'Shea. "You're probably right Eddie must have been on the Neptune all along, how he got on the ship beats me but it has to be him, it's too much of a coincidence, but Christ Almighty, how he ended up in a combat zone is something else." "But Brannigan" he continued "we have to take responsibility for the young lad we're going to get Eddie home we're working on the case right now we're going to get him released from the Vietcong, we're going to do a prisoner exchange and get him home safely to Dublin as soon as possible. I'll be in touch."

The phone went dead. Basher Brannigan finished off his whiskey in one quick gulp and headed down to the motor pool to pick up a police car, he had to find Shaky Shanahan and confirm that Eddie had a military tattoo on his arm, not that it mattered one little bit; he knew it was Eddie. He couldn't wait to give Bridie Kelly the good news, to put an end to her suffering, to tell her Eddie had been found safe and well.

After calling at several city centre pubs he finally found Shaky Shanahan in Fagan's bar in Drumcondra sitting sipping a pint of Guinness.

"Shaky it's about Eddie," he said. "Has he by any chance got an Irish Army tattoo on his arm?"

"Yeh he has a tattoo here on his arm" replied Shaky, pointing to his forearm; he got it when his brother Paddy was killed in Africa. Why? What's up? What's a tattoo got to do with anything?"

"Thank Christ for that Shaky, listen you're never going to believe this; I think they've found Eddie. No in fact I'm certain they've found Eddie, he's alive and well."Shaky looked confused.

"What do yeh mean they've found Eddie, who *are they* if I may ask". "The Yanks" replied Brannigan

Shaky nearly dropped his pint. "Jaysus Basher dat's fantastic news so it is, dat's bleedin massive. Where was he, and by the way, what's it got to do with the Yanks?"

"The Yank's found him in Vietnam," replied Basher. "In Vietnam."

"Viet-nam what?" said Shaky nearly choking on his pint. "What the fuck was Eddie doing in Vietnam?"

"He went on that American war ship: the one I told yeh about, the one that was in Dublin the night he went missing. He was on the ship all along and no one listened to me and dat's how he ended up in Vietnam"

"Come on Shaky finish up that pint will yeh for God's sake let's go up to Finglas and tell Bridie the good news."

"Yeh know what Shaky," said Brannigan as they drove towards Finglas West. "I knew there was something funny all along about this case. I knew Eddie wasn't dead or over in England, I knew he was on that fuckin American ship all along so I did".

Seamy opened the door to Basher and Shaky. "What in the name of sweet Jaysus do you pair want? Is this a bleedin joke or what? A fuckin copper and an undertaker? Sweet Jaysus what a bleedin pair – one to arrest me and one to bury me. You're like bleedin Mutt and Jeff the pair of yeh, bleedin Mutt and Jeff so yeh are," he said laughing.

"We've got fantastic news Seamy, fantastic news, by the way where's Bridie?" Shaky asked. "She's been in her bed she hasn't been well for a while now," replied Seamy.

"Get her up quick for Christ's sake. It's all over! It's all over! They've found Eddie; the Yank's found Eddie and he's alive and well."

"What do you mean the Yanks found Eddie'?"

"They found him in Hanoi over in Vietnam," said Basher Brannigan.

"Viet-bleedin'-what?" said Seamy. "Where the fuck is dat?"

"It's where the Yanks are fighting the war," replied Basher.

"Will yeh go on outa dat!" said Seamy. "Pull the other one; there's bells on it?"

"No," said Shaky, "its true Seamy. It's all true."

"What the fuck was he doing in Viet-whatever-yeh-call-it when it's at home? I thought he did a runner and was over in England with that lanky Monks fucker so I did, Jaysus, hold on a minute now. I saw that bleedin kip Vietnam where the war is on the box in the Dockers the other night; a crowd of bleedin gippos, dat's what those little fuckers are and do yeh know what? All those fucker's eat is bleedin rice. Jaysus no wonder they've got slantly bleedin eyes."

At that moment, Bridie came down the stairs in her dressing gown. When she heard the commotion she knew it was something important.

"Bridie! Bridie!" said Shaky excitedly. "It's Eddie, the Yank's found Eddie, he's alive and kicking so he is Bridie. He's coming home Bridie, isn't that great news, isn't dat just fantastic?" "Oh Sacred Heart of Jaysus," said Bridie as she fainted in a heap on the hall floor.

The Americans held several very important Vietcong high-ranking officers prisoner in Saigon (not in Sergeant Rock's marine compound) and through a Red Cross intermediary they arranged with the North Vietnamese Government in Hanoi for Eddie to be exchanged for a high-ranking Vietcong officer called Major Gip Gip. The Vietcong hadn't figured out what nationality their prisoner was; they were just glad to get Major Gip Gip released from captivity, he was one of their best field commanders and for his release they would have exchanged anyone; so they lost all interest in the unidentified prisoner.

At first light on a Monday morning two guards entered Eddie's cell, woke him and gave him some clean clothes and a basin of water with some soap. Eddie knew instinctively something was up. The guard's were usually very hostile and aggressive towards him but on this particular morning they acted very differently. He washed quickly and dressed in the army fatigues and was led to a waiting jeep. After three hour's drive they reached the Laos border where they stopped at a border crossing. A group of soldiers and couple of civilian's stood on the far side of the barrier marking the border between North Vietnam and Laos and on seeing Eddie a tall man in a dark suit and wearing sun glasses called out "Eddie, Eddie Kelly over here son". He beckoned to Eddie to cross over the checkpoint and join him. Eddie was overcome with emotion when he heard his name been called. Tom Keating shook Eddie's hand firmly. "Eddie" he said "I'm Mister Keating from the American Embassy I arranged your release son welcome home; we'll take care of you now and get you safely back to Ireland. It's all over Eddie your going home now son".

They travelled by army helicopter to Saigon and on to the C.I.A. headquarters where Eddie was kitted out in new army fatigues that fitted, fed and an army doctor tended to his wound. Eddie told the full story of his misadventures to Keating, all about Captain Grant on the ship and Sergeant Rock and how he had been beaten up and forced into the marines under the name of Private John Moran. He told Keating about the ambush in the jungle and how the Vietcong soldier's had captured him. He started to cry when he spoke about the horrible death of the young marines in the explosion and about the young girl and how she feed him and looked after his wound and how they had killed her so brutally.

Keating was dumbfounded; it just didn't make sense. Why wasn't Eddie reported by the captain as a stowaway? How did he end up in the marines? What puzzled him also was how Eddie wasn't shot dead after the ambush, who had saved him from the Vietcong? How did he get to the village? The whole thing was weird; it just didn't make any sense at all. There were so many unanswered questions.

Two days later Eddie Kelly boarded an Air France civilian aircraft on a flight to Paris where he would catch a connecting

Aer Lingus plane from Paris to Dublin. It was his first time on an aeroplane but he wasn't nervous at all. After the helicopter ride this was easy. At Charles De Gaulle airport in Paris he boarded an Aer Lingus jet bound for Dublin. When Eddie heard the young air hostess speaking in Irish before takeoff, tears ran down his cheeks. He knew his scant knowledge of the Irish language had saved him from certain death at the hands of the Vietcong.

He smiled as the plane took off thinking about how he went out for a quiet pint of Guinness on a Friday night in Dublin and ended up on a warship to Vietnam, a helicopter ride to the jungle and finally on an Irish plane flying him home to Dublin where it all begun. Eddie Kelly – man on a mission. Then he remembered that he was going home with no money except for the few dollars Mister Keating had given him. He still couldn't buy his ma the fancy grave and the marble headstone she wanted so badly. On top of that his beautiful Vietnamese girl was dead and all those poor dead soldiers from Alpha Company. The hell he'd been through in Vietnam was all for nothing; he was back to square one. Eddie Kelly – man on a mission-mission to nowhere.

FAMILY REUNIONS

Aer Lingus flight 3814 landed at Dublin airport at six a.m. on a bright Saturday morning almost eight weeks after Eddie had left his house in Finglas to go down town to the Ace of Spades for a few pints of Guinness and to meet his girlfriend and friends in the Go-Go beat club in Abbey Street. In the empty airport arrivals lounge Shaky Shanahan and Colette Murphy stood with Bridie and Seamy Kelly who were waiting for the return of their son Eddie, the accidental stowaway, from his adventure in South East Asia. Shaky had driven Bridie, Seamy and Colette to the airport in his hearse to save them the bus fare. Just before the plane landed Basher Brannigan and John O'Shay from the American Embassy joined them. They eagerly awaited the arrival of Eddie Kelly; they wanted to see the young lad in the flesh. O'Shea had been ordered to carry out a full-scale investigation into the whole Kelly affair by his superiors in Washington.

Bridie couldn't believe her eyes when she spotted Eddie as he walked through the arrivals gate, he looked totally different with his shaved head and dressed in green army fatigues, he looked every bit the soldier. He was no longer a boy; her baby boy was a man, her little funny cuts Eddie Kelly.

When he saw his mother Eddie burst into tears and ran to embrace her crying, "Mammy, I'm home, I'm sorry about everything, but I'm home now. It was all a terrible accident, a terrible mistake." Seamy nodded at Eddie. "Well at least yeh got yer fuckin hair cut pal, but I'll tell yeh something for nuthin; the bleedin slanty eyed gippo barber did yeh no fuckin favours so he didn't." Then he looked closely at his son to see if he was carrying any bags that might have drink, cigarettes or something of value from Vietnam. He wondered what sort of gargle the little slanty-eyes drank. Seamy was disappointed; Eddie had nothing, only the green army fatigues he was dressed in and a pair of black shiny Army boots.

Colette Murphy embraced Eddie passionately; he looked so handsome in the military fatigues. She was so excited; she couldn't wait. She had big plans, very big plans for her accidental stowaway, very big plans indeed.

Eddie turned to Shaky. "I'm sorry about all this, Shaky so I am. I never meant it to happen and I suppose you've given me job to someone else."

"No son no. I would never have done dat. I always knew something happened to you, I always knew you would come home. Listen Eddie , I want to introduce you to the man who is responsible for you being here today, Eddie this is Detective Basher Brannigan; he's the one who got you home son – him and Mister O'Shea from the American Embassy." Basher Brannigan shook Eddie's hand warmly. "Welcome home son, welcome home. Jaysus Eddie you led me on a merry trail halfway around the world so yeh did. Anyway I'm glad you're home safe and sound and by the way", he said smiling, "I'm glad yeh got your hair cut over in Vietnam it looks very smart, very smart indeed. "Eddie" he continued, "I want you meet Mister O Shay from the American Embassy."

John O'Shea shook Eddie's hand. "Welcome home son. Eddie listen, I want you and your folks to come out to the embassy with me, we'll get some breakfast. I need to talk about what happened to you, I want you to tell me the whole story – everything you told Mister Keating. Is that okay Eddie? The embassy car is outside".

"Sure Mister O' Shea. By the way sir, will we get coffee and those flapjacks with maple syrup?"

"Sure son sure; anything you want, complements of Uncle Sam."

At the embassy Eddie told the story again to John O'Shay. How he had met an American sailor, Jerome, in his local pub and how he had brought him onboard the warship the USS Neptune. O'Shea was shocked when Eddie told him about Captain Grant and especially about Master Sergeant Rock and the way they had treated him. John O'Shea was visibly shaken by Eddie's story: how a young Irish civilian was taken to Vietnam and then forced into the Marine Corps and sent into active service, wounded and nearly killed. It was an amazing story, absolutely incredible. "Listen, Eddie," John O'Shea said, "I promise you heads are going to roll over this whole affair. I'm going to contact the American Embassy in Saigon and get to the bottom of this whole sorry mess. Okay Eddie? Leave it with me and I'll get back to you. I promise you, son; someone will pay for what happened to you this will go right to the top son."

John O'Shea was furious at the way the young lad had been treated and nearly killed. He paced up and the down the floor seething with anger. *This is an absolute outrage; Grant and Rock have to get a dishonourable discharge for their* gross *misconduct* the thought now *to get to the bottom of this mess and nail the two bastards.* He immediately contacted Tom Keating at the American Embassy in Saigon and asked him to carry out a full-scale investigation into Captain Grant of the USS Neptune; he should have reported the stowaway to his superiors and the Irish Authorities immediately at least his mother would have known where he was. And then there was Master Sergeant Fred Rock of the United States Marine Corps; he was the real culprit of the whole sorry affair. He falsified army documents for his own gain and sent a non-American civilian with no military experience into a war zone. Rock could have easily had young Eddie Kelly killed in combat and he nearly did. John O'Shay instructed Tom Keating to go aboard the USS Neptune in Saigon Bay where the ship was on patrol duty since Eddie's disembarkation and interview all the sailor's onboard regarding the stowaway. Then it was on to the marine compound in Saigon to speak to Sergeant Rock and investigate the file on Private John Moran – alias Eddie Kelly. It was vital that they got all the necessary proof to charge Grant and Rock with gross misconduct and get them dishonourably discharged from their posts. It wouldn't help Eddie Kelly but at least justice would be done.

Just after dawn the following morning, Tom Keating and two secret service agents went aboard the USS Neptune and despite Captain Grant's protestations interviewed each of the crew about Eddie Kelly. Keating was very surprised to find that many of the men knew nothing about the stowaway. Later on he spoke to Jerome King. Jerome knew something was wrong; he was sure that if Eddie had got home safely that would have been the end of the matter but he knew something was amiss; he knew something must have happened to Eddie when he went ashore.

"What's happened to Eddie, sir?" asked Jerome. "Something serious must be wrong. Did he not get home safely, sir? When he left the ship he was to be sent back to Ireland. What happened, sir?"

When Keating did not answer the question, Jerome thought he was in serious trouble with the navy for bringing Eddie Kelly aboard the ship.

"Listen Mister Keating," continued Jerome "when we docked in Dublin I went up the town for a drink and met Eddie Kelly in a pub, it was my entire fault, sir, I took him aboard the ship and I take full responsibility for my actions sir. Please don't let anything happen to Eddie Kelly. He's a good guy. He's my buddy and I'll take the blame for what's happened sir"

Keating was impressed by Jerome's loyalty to Eddie. "Look Jerome." He said, "I appreciate your honesty son, so what I'm going to tell you now is confidential. Eddie Kelly is safely back in Dublin; he got home two days ago."

Jerome was shocked. "What do you mean 'two days ago', sir? He left the ship well over three weeks ago. What happened to him? Where was he sir?"

Keating didn't answer but Jerome knew by his face that something had happened to Eddie on shore.

"Sir when Eddie left the ship three weeks ago he was told he was to be sent home to Ireland. Why did he only get home two days ago?"

"I can't answer that son," replied Keating as he turned and left the ship.

Jerome called after him. "Sir can you answer me one thing? Am I going to get in trouble over taking a civilian onboard the ship?"

"No son. The case is closed, over, finished; it's the last you'll ever hear of your Irish buddy Eddie Kelly."

Back at C.I.A. headquarters Keating wrote up his report then rang the naval police and ordered the immediate arrest of Captain Grant and First Officer Peters.

Later that day Keating drove down to the military compound at Saigon docks to talk to Master Sergeant Freddie Rock. Rock was in the process of clearing out his office, his packed kit was stacked in a corner; he was flying home that night.

"Going somewhere sergeant?" asked Keating.

"Stateside sir," replied Rock grinning. "This man's war is over. I'm flying home tonight. Anyway what can I do for you, sir?" Rock asked sarcastically.

"Sergeant Rock, I want to talk to you about a Private John Moran."

Rock froze in his chair; he knew he had a serious situation on his hands. "What about Private Moran?" Rock replied coldly. "He's dead: killed in action about three or four weeks ago; whole patrol blown off the face of the earth by the little yellow slanty eyed fuckers; never had a chance, poor bastards. All we found were body parts and dog tags. Hold on sir." Rock called in the young private. "Get me the file on Private John Moran."

"Right away sir."

"Anyway sir what's all this about Moran?"

"Nothing sergeant; just some routine enquiries. Nothing important."

"Here sir." The young Private handed Keating the file. "I'm sure everything is in order, sir," said Rock, a faint grin on his face. Rock felt confident they'd find nothing. He'd made sure that all the paperwork was in order.

The file contained details of Moran's background; he was from New York and was conscripted into the marines and had completed his marine training successfully in Paris Island.

Keating was surprised; Moran had listed his nationality as Irish. In fact he had been conscripted into the marines only a year after he had arrived in New York from Ireland. Moran was Irish; the same as Eddie Kelly.

Rock knew instinctively that Keating had seen something in the file but so what? There was no way he could prove anything especially with Kelly, eh Moran, dead, killed in action, Rock corrected himself mentally, a grin on his face.

Keating continued to read the file. Moran had deserted on arrival in Vietnam and was recaptured and redeployed with the Marine Corps the same night Eddie Kelly arrived on the USS Neptune from Dublin. But that proved nothing. Keating knew that Rock would have covered his tracks well. The file stated that Moran had been handed over from detention by Rock to the marines and resumed active service but was killed by an explosion in a Vietcong ambush in the northern sector. His remains were not recovered but his dog tags were found. The paperwork seemed to be in order.

Keating opened the sealed envelope in the file which was marked K.I.A. and held the blood-stained dog tags in his hands – 'Private John Moran, U.S. Marine Corps. He carefully placed the dog tags back in the envelope. Keating knew he had to find something concrete, then he found it: it was the last piece of paper in the file – a key document that Rock had missed. It was all that Keating needed to nail Rock. The paper read:

In case of my death during active service or capture by the enemy, I decree that my army pay, severance and all pension monies owed to me as a soldier under active duty in South East Asia, serving in the United States Marine Corps, is paid to the following beneficiary:

Mrs Bridie Kelly
38 Kildonan Parade
Finglas West
Dublin
Ireland

It was the standard federal insurance form that combat soldiers signed before active service. Eddie Kelly was afraid to sign his own name on the document in case he got a beating from

Sergeant Rock; so, instead, he signed the name John Moran, but his named beneficiary was his mother. Only Eddie Kelly could have signed the papers. It was conclusive proof; Rock must have overlooked the document. What a stroke of good luck.

Christ thought Keating, *Eddie Kelly's mum Bridie would receive his full K.I.A. monies and the life insurance payment. Nobody could stop the payments. It was all legal. John Moran was killed in action and she was the legally named beneficiary – case closed. Leave well enough alone. At least young Kelly would get some money out of this whole crazy incident. He deserved it – moral justice.*

Keating turned to Rock, who knew by Keating's face that he'd found something important.

"File in order, sir?"

"Not exactly. Can you explain this, sergeant?" He handed Sergeant Rock the papers Eddie Kelly had signed in Moran's name, naming Bridie Kelly as the beneficiary

Rock froze when he saw the form. He knew exactly what it meant. How could he have missed it, how could he have been so stupid. His gut hurt. He knew it was all over. He knew he was fucked; he had a situation on his hands, a very serious situation indeed. Jesus he never thought it would end like this – all because of some good-for-nothing, long-haired fucking Irish hippie freak.

"Private," ordered Keating, "call the military police. Master Sergeant Fredrick Rock, you're under arrest for gross misconduct. You're in serious trouble Mister Rock, serious trouble indeed."

AIRMAIL

Early one Friday morning the postman handed a large special delivery envelope to Bridie Kelly. The envelope was covered with American airmail stamps and Bridie was puzzled; she knew nobody in the United States.

After a cup of tea and a cigarette she gathered up the courage to open the sealed envelope. The envelope contained a cheque and an official-looking letter from the United States Government. Bridie didn't quite understand what it all meant. The letter stated:

To the beneficiary of Private, First Class, Marine Corps, John Moran;

Find enclosed a United States Government endorsed cheque in the sum of two thousand US Dollars, payable to the above-named legal beneficiary, owing to the death of Private Moran on active service in South East Asia.

The beneficiary will also receive Private Moran's monthly pension allowance, payable until the death of the beneficiary in the monthly sum of one hundred U S Dollars.

Signed
Secretary of Defence
U. S. Government Treasury Department

Bridie was shocked. What the hell was a beneficiary? She could hardly read the word but the cheque was made out in her name and it had something to do with a Private John Moran. Who the hell was Private John Moran? She knew it must have something to do with Eddie and the war in Vietnam.

Eddie had said he was forced to be a Private Moran in Vietnam but why did the American Government send the money to her.

She quickly put on her coat and caught the bus down to Shanahan's funeral parlour in Finlater's Place. When she showed Eddie the cheque he couldn't believe his eyes. He had seen a few cheques before but never for so much money. When he read the letter he understood what it was all about. In Vietnam the quartermaster had asked him to sign an insurance form naming someone to receive his pay, pension and insurance money if he was killed in action. He had named his mother on the form. He'd signed John Moran's name because he was afraid of Sergeant Rock and that's what had happened. To the American Army John Moran was killed in action; that's why they sent a cheque to Bridie Kelly the named beneficiary. Eddie couldn't believe it – so much money.

"Ma," he said excitedly, "Sweet Jaysus yeh know what this means Ma, don't yeh?"

"Yes," replied Bridie with a look of bewilderment on her face. "I know, I know son," she answered excitedly, tears running down her face. "We can have fish and chips for dinner every night of the week."

"No," said Eddie, laughing. "No Ma. It's better than a poke in the eye with a sharp stick; at last we can make all your dreams come true. We can get you dat fancy grave and big marble statue at the front of Glasnevin cemetery for Paddy. At last Ma you can have what you always wanted more than anything else in the whole world"

"Eddie! Eddie!" said Bridie, crying. "You were always special. I always knew you'd make me dreams come true son. Come over here and give your ould mammy a big hug, me little funny cuts, Eddie Kelly."

The last time Eddie had seen his mother so happy was when he was a child with Paddy playing on Sandymount strand on their day trips to the beach during the summer holidays.

Shaky used his contact in the registrar's office at Glasnevin cemetery and was able, with not a small amount of difficulty, to get a burial plot right at the front of the graveyard beside the main road and adjacent to the graves of all the famous Irish patriots just as Bridie always wanted. It cost a tidy sum but was worth every penny. He then commissioned a friend of his who was a stone mason in Stoneybatter, on

Bridie's behalf; to carve a white marble statue of Cuchulain for the new grave with the inscriptions' she'd wanted.

But he still had some unfinished business to attend to. He knew how much Bridie wanted the grave and the headstone, and that was done, but there was something very important, something else he had to attend to. That night he went down to the Bridewell with a bottle of Powers whiskey for Basher Brannigan. He poured a large measure of whiskey into each of the tea stained mugs and handed one to Brannigan. "Listen Basher I want to thank yeh for getting Eddie home safe and sound. If it wasn't for you we might have never got him home alive and dat's a fact so it is. So now detective I'll raise me glass to yeh so I will. Good luck to yeh now and may the road always rise to meet yeh and may yeh be safely in heaven Mister Brannigan before the devil knows your dead. Basher Brannigan God bless yeh now for all you've done for the Kelly family. God bless yeh detective"

Basher Brannigan was moved. "Jaysus Shaky. Don't get all sentimental on me now. It was nuthin'," he replied, embarrassment in his voice. "I was glad to help poor Bridie Kelly; it was the least I could do. And yeh know what Shaky; if it wasn't for dem fuckin Yanks the whole sorry episode would never have happened. I fuckin knew Eddie was on that ship all along so I did and they just wouldn't listen to me."

"Dat's what I want to talk to yeh about Basher – the Yanks they nearly got Eddie killed didn't they. Okay, Eddie's getting a few Yankee dollars or at least Bridie is but they still owe Eddie don't they Basher."

"What are yeh on about   Shaky? What do yeh want off the Yanks for Eddie?"

"Well it's not for Eddie exactly as such – more for Bridie. I've got the plot Bridie always wanted in Glasnevin cemetery. Jaysus Basher that was hard enough so it was, had to pull in a few favours and promise a certain person (no name, no shame) a few bob on the side to secure the plot, but that's okay it's a done deal so it is and the marble statue is being carved as we speak dat was no problem. However let's get down to the important business now. I want to get Paddy a full military funeral, all the trappings, yeh know? The marching soldiers, shots over the grave, army bugler playing the last post – all the schoolboy stuff. I know Bridie will love all dat so she will. But there's something else Basher, listen to me very carefully now; it's something very important so it is. I'd love to be able to get the remains of Bridie's father Christy taken out of dat ould English military graveyard up at dat Arbour Hill place and buried with Paddy in Glasnevin with a full military funeral. Wouldn't that be just great Basher? Fantastic for Bridie to be able to give her poor father a proper Christian burial."Basher looked at Shaky with astonishment. "Shaky, hold on a minute now, if you think I can arrange dat yeh must be bleedin joking, they'd laugh at me so they would I'm only a humble detective so I am."

"Basher you're no humble detective so you're not, you're the best detective in the city of Dublin so yeh are, didn't I just tell yeh? We're yeh not listening to what I said? Eddie Kelly would be dead now if it wasn't for you Basher." Shaky raised his glass again to Brannigan. "But you're right, be Jaysus; we'll have to pull a few strings on this one so we will, now dat's where the Yanks come in so they do," Shaky continued. "Yeh probably read it in the Herald; the government's trying to get American companies to set up their businesses in Ireland and get some employment here to stop all the young people having to emigrate to America and England to find work." Basher Brannigan was puzzled. "And what in God's name has that got to do with Eddie Kelly?"

"Your man in the embassy – O'Shea. He's the one who wouldn't listen to you about Eddie being on the ship wasn't he? Give him a call, put a bit of pressure on him, tell him yeh need a few favours."

Without hesitation Brannigan picked up the phone and called O'Shea. "Listen chief, I blame you for Eddie Kelly nearly getting killed so I do. Yeh wouldn't listen to me when I told yeh the young lad was on the ship so now I want you to arrange a few things for me just to square things up so to speak." Brannigan told him what he wanted.

O'Shea was surprised at Brannigan's demands but the next day he contacted the Minister of Defence and using the considerable influence of the American Administration with the Irish Government arranged to have the remains of Volunteer Christopher Kelly, Dublin Citizen's Army (or what remained of him, to be precise, after fifty-one years) exhumed from Arbour Hill cemetery and a full military funeral for both him and his grandson, Private Patrick Christopher Kelly.

But there was one more little thing Brannigan wanted O'Shea to arrange.

PIGS CAN FLY

Just under a year or so after Eddie Kelly had accidentally stowed away on the United States warship the USS Neptune he stood dressed in his new black suit, shiny winkle picker boots and slim black tie at the front of Glasnevin Cemetery with his family and friends. He even got his long hair trimmed for the occasion.

They stood beside the fancy grave Shaky had purchased on behalf of Bridie right at the front of the cemetery beside the main road and next to the graves of all the famous Irish patriots. It was a beautiful grave with a fine big white marble statue of Cuchulain – the fallen Irish hero and even bigger than the statue in the GPO.

There were two inscribed plaques just below the statue. One read:

Private Paddy Christopher Kelly, 5th Infantry Company, Padraig Pearse Battalion, Eastern Command, Irish Defence Forces. Killed in the service of his country in Katanga, 1964. Oglaigh na hEireann.

The second plaque read:

Volunteer Christy Doyle, Dublin City Brigade, Irish Citizen's Army. Killed in action fighting for Irish freedom and the working class, Easter 1916. Drong Atha Cliath Oglaigh na h Eireann.

It was a beautiful summer's day in Glasnevin cemetery on that special Friday afternoon in July as Bridie Kelly's life-long dream came true. Tears of sadness and joy ran down her cheeks as she stood by the open graveside of her eldest son and her father. Her brother Sean stood beside her. He had come back to Ireland for the first time since he emigrated to Manchester over forty years before and had come home to bury his father, his sister's eldest son and the ghosts of the past. They had waited all their lives to see their father get a proper Christian burial and now he finally was.

Seamy stood at the back of the gathered crowd chatting with Fibber O'Toole.

"Jaysus Seamy me ould flower" said Fibber, "yeh must be a very happy man what with the day dat's in it."

"Happy Fibber? I'm more than bleedin happy pal; I'm over the bleedin moon so I am, over the fuckin moon pal. Jaysus what a session we're going to have when the formalities are over. Around to the Gravediggers for gargle, gargle and more gargle and yeh know what Fibber we won't have to dip our hand in our pocket if yeh know what I mean, bleedin massive so it is, bleedin massive"

They both rubbed their hands in glee, giggling like little children.

Mary O'Toole stood behind Bridie with her six children lined up in descending order, like toy soldiers, dressed in their best Sunday clothes, her eldest son Anto with his arm affectionately around his best friend Eddie.

Colette arrived with Imelda and Mickser. Imelda was eight month's pregnant.

Shaky approached Bridie in a quiet dignified manner his top hat clutched in his hands. "Bridie God bless yeh missus. I'm glad everything came right in the end. Yeh waited a long time for this special day so yeh did, I'm very happy for yeh now so I am."

Bridie turned to Shaky. "Shaky I know this wonderful day is all because of you – your kindness. How can I ever thank yeh for all you've done for Eddie and for me?"

"Bridie your father gave his life trying to help the poor working people of Dublin
and it was a very brave and noble thing to do; the least he deserves is a bit of recognition for his sacrifice and a decent Christian burial to boot.

Sergeant Molloy stood beside Father O'Donohue at the graveside. "Great day Father," he said, "great day for a funeral so it is."

"So it is Sergeant. So it is. Incredible how God always finds a way, quite incredible. It's Buddhist philosophy so it is; they call it the *Law of Attraction* or *Law of Resonance* something like that so they do"

Eddie nearly fell into the open grave in shock when he saw the two black American sailors make their way through the large crowd towards the grave. It was Jerome and Sonny. The USS Neptune had docked the day before and O'Shea had arranged everything under a little pressure from Basher Brannigan.

The arrival of the USS Neptune in Dublin was the hardest thing to organise. The arrangements with the Irish Government were easy apart from the use of the Citizen's Army flag. For some reason, which O'Shea couldn't understand, the Irish Government weren't happy about the use of the Starry Plough flag draped over Christy Doyle's coffin. They would have preferred it if the coffin was draped in the tricolour of the Irish Republic but Basher Brannigan was insistent. O'Shea never quite got to grips with the intricacy of Irish politics.

The date of the burials had been scheduled around the arrival of the USS Neptune sailing home to the States after a twelve-month tour of duty in South East Asia; the Captain of the ship was not William Grant.

A small elderly man, who had medals pinned to his chest, came up to Bridie. "Bridie," he said, "you don't know me Bridie I was with your father Christy when he was killed in the G.P.O. in the Easter Rising fighting with Jem Connolly. He died in me arms so he did. May the lord above have mercy on his poor unfortunate soul? I remember his last words as if it was yesterday; He was critically wounded and as he lay they're dying he cried out for his wife and children and his final words were, 'Nora, forgive me' so they were Bridie."

Bridie was speechless.

"Me name is Brendan Mackey Bridie. I was a volunteer in the Dublin Brigade of the Citizen's Army with your father and we used to work together in the tram company" he continued. "This is the happiest day of my life seeing your father my comrade getting a proper Christian burial after all these long years." Tears ran down Brendan Mackey's face as he hugged Bridie. "He died a soldier Bridie. He died for our freedom, to free our country from the English, so he did and now he's finally getting the proper Christian burial he deserves – a soldier's burial."

The crowd went silent as the colour party of the Irish Army approached the graveside bearing the two coffins: Private Paddy Kelly's coffin draped in the Irish tricolour and Volunteer Christy Doyle's coffin draped in the Starry Plough. As the two coffins were lowered into the grave an army bugler played the last post for the two fallen soldiers and a volley of shots was fired over the grave as a final salute. The Commanding Officer presented Bridie with the carefully folded tricolour, the Starry Plough flag and a war of independence service medal for Volunteer Christy Doyle. To Eddie's amazement John O'Shea stepped forward and presented him with a folded flag of the United States of America and a Vietnam service medal which he pinned to Eddie's chest. The two sailors saluted Eddie as he stood by the graveside of his brother and his grandfather, proud as punch – three Irish heroes.

At that moment, a packed number forty bus stopped outside the main gates of the cemetery.

"Jaysus," said an old man, "what the feck is going on in there with all dem soldiers and all dat?"

"Ah Jaysus," an old woman replied, "dat's the new statue for Bridie Kelly's son; yeh know him, yer man yeh him dat was killed out there in Africa in the army and eaten by dem Balubas. Yeh Paddy Kelly eaten by Balubas for Ireland so he was. Ah Jaysus will yeh look over there look, for Jaysus sake over there, beside the grave. It's dem black fellas, Jaysus; even the Balubas must have come over to Ireland for the bleedin funeral."

Nosey Mc Dowell was lurking in the background. *Jaysus,* he thought, *what a scoop, what a fuckin scoop for tonight's edition of the Evening Herald.*

"Eddie," said Jerome, "fancy coming onboard the ship tonight for a few beers just for old time's sake?"

Eddie stood in disbelief. "Jaysus yeh must be bleedin jokin. The last time I went onboard your feckin ship I ended up halfway across the world fighting in Vietnam in Uncle Sam's Army and I've got the medal to prove it and a bullet hole to boot. No thanks pal my fighting days are over so they are, but I tell yeh what; let's all go around to the Gravediggers for a few pints of Guinness. Jerome yeh remember the black stuff yeh liked so much your first night in Dublin remember in the Ace of Spades?"

"Hey Sonny," shouted Jerome. "You're gonna taste that black beer, Guinness, I was telling you about on the ship."

As they walked the short distance from the cemetery to the Gravediggers public house, up the narrow lane, Eddie carefully took off the Vietnamese service medal that John O'Shea had pinned on his chest. He looked closely at the small medal that he held in his hand: a small triangular bit of cloth with red stripes on a yellow background and a plastic coin with the words 'The Republic of Vietnam' on the front and 'The United States of America' on the back.

Christ, he thought, *is this all a human life is worth? A cheap plastic medal like this?*

Then he thought about   the American soldiers in Alpha Company the day of the explosion and their screams and cries for their mothers. It was something he would never forget until the day he died. Tears ran down his face.

I'll say a prayer for them at mass on Sunday, he thought, wiping the tears from his face with his sleeve. Then Eddie wondered what ever happened to the real Private John Moran whose medal he was holding in his hand. If John Moran hadn't deserted from the marines he would have never ended up in the jungle carrying a rifle and nearly getting killed. He'd have been sent straight back home and that would be the end of the story. But then again, he thought, if it hadn't happened he'd never have got to meet the girl of his dreams and get the American money to buy the fancy grave and marble statue for Paddy. His grandfather would never have got a proper burial and, most importantly of all, to be able to make his mother's dream come true – all thanks to the deserter Private John Moran. Pigs can fly!

EPILOGUE

With her monthly cheque from the United States Government Bridie, for the first time in her life, had plenty of money. She renovated the house, bought a television set, a fridge, and made sure that she always had plenty of food, the fire was always lit in winter and the rent was always paid on time. She even stopped buying pig's feet and tripe.

All of Paddy's belongings – his uniform, the gun and medals – were carefully stored away in a box and put up in the attic. His bedroom was turned into a spare room for Eddie's kids Jerome and Sonny, named after their fathers' sailor friends, when they came to stay with their grandmother.

Bridie was the happiest women in Ireland, her father and her eldest son were finally laid to rest and she had finally found peace of mind all thanks to her beloved son Eddie and his amazing adventure. There was always something very special about her son, little funny cuts, Eddie Kelly.

A year or so after big Frankie Coyle the bouncer had put the two hippies in hospital with serious injuries (as a result of multiple hammer blows and stab wounds from a broken bottle) it was payback time for the hippies. One Friday just before midnight they got hold of a shotgun and drove up in an old Ford Transit van to the Go-Go club in Abbey Street. When they pulled up outside the club they called big Frankie over.

"What's the story pal, what's up?" were Frankie's last words before one of the hippies fired the shotgun at point blank range into his chest. He ended up in a wheelchair for the rest of his days. The hippies were never caught.

Sergeant Molloy from Finglas Garda station was called to a domestic dispute up in the estate late on a Saturday night. As a drunken husband attacked his wife with a knife, Sergeant

Molloy stepped in between the couple to protect the woman and was fatally stabbed in the heart.

The band from Limerick, Grannies Intentions, went on to be the first Irish band to get a major record deal from Decca Records in London. Their first single reached the top twenty in the pop charts in England and was a big hit in Ireland. Johnny Duhan (not Dunne as big Frankie had called him) left the band and became one of Ireland's most creative songwriters, writing beautiful but sad songs, and now lives in Galway. Johnny Duhan's most famous ballad is called 'The Voyage', and is sure to be played at all weddings in Ireland and became Eddie's favourite song for obvious reasons. The Voyage was played at Eddie's wedding.

One Friday after Bridie cashed in her American cheque at the General Post Office Seamy stole ten pounds from her purse and headed down to his favourite watering hole, the Dockers, to meet his fellow moochers. In a drunken stupor on the way home he stopped to urinate into the river Liffey. He stumbled in the darkness and fell into the river while he was trying to do up his flies and was drowned. A very strange thing was that; not one of the moochers, not even one of Seamy's bosom companions, went to the funeral. They were too busy drinking in the Dockers or in some other public house in the city of Dublin. Moochers didn't like funerals much – too much reality gave them the willies.

One evening, after a funeral in Glasnevin Cemetery, Eddie as usual went home to his wife and kids in Finglas. Since he got married he stopped going into the pub every night after work for a drink but Shaky Shanahan hadn't. He called into to the Gravedigger's public house and ordered a double Powers whiskey. He took one gulp of the whiskey and dropped dead with the glass still clutched in his hand. They say he died with a smile on his face.

After spending a long winter's night in the city morgue with the body of a fourteen-year-old pregnant girl who was fished out of the river Liffey, Basher Brannigan went home to his lodgings in Drumcondra. He felt unwell all night and thought he had the flu. He drank several hot whiskeys and went to bed. His landlady found him dead the next morning.

John O'Shea was transferred from the American Embassy in Dublin to Saigon. One night he was assassinated by the Vietcong as he left the American Embassy. The leader of the assassination squad was Major Gip Gip the Vietcong prisoner who had been exchanged for Eddie Kelly.

Captain Grant of the USS Neptune received a dishonourable discharge from the navy and ended up the captain of a pleasure steamer on the Mississippi river. He never got to make Admiral and he never got to visit the old country again.

First Officer Peters received a dishonourable discharge from the navy and now works in New York as an insurance salesman. He's still an idiot.

Master Sergeant Freddie 'not so lucky' Rock was court marshalled and dishonourably discharged from the United States Army. He now works as a security guard in a Wal-Mart somewhere in the Southern States of America. He never got the young thing to keep him warm at night or the big fancy television set. He ended his long career in the army the way he had begun all those long years before – penniless.

John O'Shay took great pleasure in watching Rock lose everything.

As Rock left the military courtroom after his court marshal, O'Shea shouted to Rock, "Hey, sergeant. Sorry – Mister Rock. Eddie Kelly, the Irish guy. You remember him? The one you nearly got killed in Vietnam? He sends his regards."

"God-damned, Irish hippy freak," was Rock's muted reply.

Jerome and Sonny were promoted to the highest rank in the United States Navy below a commissioned Officer – Master Chief – and are still serving aboard the Neptune.

Father Michael O'Donohue, the Jesuit priest who had tried to help Bridie Kelly, fell in love with one of his parishioners and left the priesthood shortly afterwards. He's now married with two children and lectures in Theology at Trinity College Dublin.

The deserter from the US Marine Corps Private John Moran had bribed the South Vietnamese guards to escape from the military stockade just as Sergeant Rock had guessed. He crossed the Cambodian border and hid out with a group of American deserters in a small village. As the deserters were arrested one by one Private John Moran just couldn't understand why he wasn't picked up by the military police. After a year he was bored and lonely and became heavily addicted to drugs. He didn't care if he was recaptured by the military police; it just didn't matter anymore. He finally left his jungle hideout and travelled to the northern port of Hue where he boarded a French ship working his passage to Canada.

Six months later he arrived back in New York City where he always expected to be arrested as a deserter but it never happened and he could never understand why he wasn't he picked up? He just didn't understand? He was always on edge, looking over his shoulder, waiting for the knock on the door, the knock that never came. He never quite came to terms with his situation, why didn't the military police track him down; he knew the marines always got their man.

He eventually joined the police force in New York and had a successful career as a detective in the vice squad. Nobody ever told John Moran that he had been killed in action serving in Uncle Sam's Army in South East Asia.

In Arlington Cemetery a name is inscribed on the wall of honour; it reads:

Private John Moran, Private First Class, Marine Corps. Killed in action, Bein Gap, 1967.

With the money left over after buying the grave at the front of Glasnevin Cemetery and the fancy marble statue Eddie invested what was left of the money in Shaky Shanahan's funeral home.

They were able to refurbish the dilapidated building and buy a new hearse. The business became more successful and a couple of years later, Eddie who became the owner after Shaky died, opened a second funeral parlour in Finglas village. The same year Eddie married Colette Murphy and they had two sons which they called Jerome and Sonny (forever ensuring that their two sons would be the source of constant ridicule because of their strange names) Eddie's sailor friends Jerome and Sonny flew to Ireland from the United States to be the best men at the wedding in the Star of the Sea church in Sandymount and they both looked splendid, dressed in their Master' Chiefs uniforms.

To this day Eddie Kelly always carried his Vietnamese service medal in his wallet and after a few pints of Guinness in his favourite pub, the Ace of Spades in town, or in his local, the Drake Inn in Finglas village he proudly tells anyone who is willing to listen about his amazing adventure all those many years ago and how he served in Uncle Sam's Army in Vietnam, fighting the communists, fighting for the free world – Irelands only representative in the Vietnam war. To prove his point and show that he is telling the truth he shows off his Vietnam service medal and sometimes when he's drunk enough he even pulls down his trousers and points to the faded scar of the bullet wound he took from a Vietcong AK 47. Every now and again he looks at his reflection in the mirror behind the bar to see if Jerome is standing behind him inviting him on his amazing adventure. Sometimes, especially at Christmas when he's drunk half a dozen pints of Guinness and a few Powers whiskeys with peppermint, he looks in the mirror and sees the face of the beautiful young Vietnamese girl – his first real love – smiling back at him: that same beautiful girl with the dark skin and the long black hair just like in his dreams. He never even knew her name. Eddie Kelly never did have that same wonderful dream again.

THE END